Sex, Love, and a

Purple Bikini

By Cheryl Brooks

Derrymane
Press

Sex, Love, and a Purple Bikini
Cheryl Brooks
Published by Derrymane Press
Copyright 2015 Cheryl Brooks
Cover by Kendra Egert

The characters and events portrayed in this book are fictitious or are used fictitiously. Any similarity to real persons, living or dead, is purely coincidental and not intended by the author.

www.cherylbrooksonline.com

Chapter 1

What happens at the beach doesn't always stay at the beach...

ഇൗൠ

New York City, June, 2007

Terri Marshall normally had no difficulty living up to her reputation as the best assistant Jacqueline Tremaine ever had, but upon occasion, she gave in to the prodding of her evil genie and did something perfectly *wicked.* Recognizing Benjamin Tremaine's voice, she hadn't bothered to ask who was on the line. She'd simply informed him that his wife was about to leave for a conference in Myrtle Beach and put the call straight through. Then she used her most reliable method for witnessing the ensuing fireworks.

After filling her watering can, Terri silently entered Jacqueline's spacious, ultra-modern office and set about tending the plants. Normally, she would have screened the call, thus saving Jacqueline from a tricky discussion with her husband, but that same evil genie had convinced her that this was one call Jacqueline ought to take.

Terri wasn't worried that she would lose her job over this lapse in judgment because for some inexplicable reason, Jacqueline considered her to be irreplaceable—a notion that probably had more to do with the fact that no one else wanted the job than any expertise on Terri's part. Jacqueline wasn't referred to as "The Boss from Hell" for nothing. There'd even been reports that some of her previous secretaries had feigned incompetence, hoping to get fired.

Terri had one advantage over her predecessors. No matter how many snide remarks or snappy comebacks ran through her head, they never showed in her face. Her own mother had often expressed difficulty in reading Terri's naturally neutral expression. However, she had no other fault to find with her enigmatic daughter. Terri's grades had always been good, and if she was disturbingly quiet at times, she had never gotten into any kind of trouble whatsoever, not even with boys.

Contrary to popular belief, she wasn't without feelings; she was simply too damn good at hiding them, possibly stemming from an inherent fear of letting them show. She couldn't recall the turn of events responsible for this peculiar quirk, but she knew that it must have been significant. She liked to think that when she was a tiny mote of genetic material drifting about in her mother's ovaries, some virus had bullied her into perpetual silence, and the addition of her father's DNA had done nothing to foster her courage. She had no way of knowing how true this was, but she did know that internalizing her feelings was so much a part of her nature as to have surely been determined prior to her birth.

Nor did she ever argue or protest when asked to do the impossible. She simply said, "I'll take care of it," and proceeded to do just that. Jacqueline clearly appreciated a woman who took action rather than wasting time arguing. However, Terri suspected that this appreciation also stemmed from the fact that she was as plain as her ruthless boss was beautiful.

If she was plain and boring on the surface, Terri's private thoughts had always kept her well entertained. In fact, she considered her reticence a plus, for she knew that if she'd voiced even a fraction of those same thoughts over the years, she would have surely been murdered by now.

Thus, it was with that same apparent lack of feeling that Terri had helped Jacqueline keep her husband at bay, although lately she'd begun to feel some pity toward Benjamin Tremaine. Even though she had never met him, she felt that no man deserved to be stuck in such a sterile, loveless marriage as theirs must be. On the other hand, if Ben was the sort who was attracted to power and success, Jacqueline was a perfect match for him.

Cold, calculating, and completely self-absorbed, Jacqueline was the ultimate executive. What was good for the company was good for her—and vice-versa. When *The Devil Wears Prada* had been released the previous summer, Terri had gone to see it three times. The resemblance between Meryl Streep's character and Jacqueline was uncanny, although their tactics differed slightly. Never nasty— she seemed to consider it beneath her—Jacqueline was unflinchingly charming and polite, and was usually smiling as she sank her claws deeply and inextricably into an adversary's back. *Don't get mad, get even* was her motto, and she lived by it.

Jacqueline's career was her top priority, and if she owed her success more to determination than brains, well, Terri was there to take up the slack, seeing to all the little details her boss might have missed. She was Jacqueline's right-hand man, her girl Friday, and her mother all rolled into one. But sometimes that evil genie got in the way...

"What do you mean, you're coming with me?" Jacqueline snapped. "I doubt you can even get a flight!" She paused, listening, her carefully makeup-enhanced eyes widening in horror, as stricken as if she'd taken a stiletto to the ribs. "You have? Well, that's, that's...wonderful! Whatever made you decide to come along?"

Terri knew better than to believe Jacqueline's feigned delight, and it was a safe bet that Ben hadn't been fooled, either. With a barely suppressed smile, she went on with her task, watering the philodendron before moving on to the next thirsty plant.

"Now, you know Terri will be there too," Jacqueline said, sounding carefully casual. "I couldn't *possibly* function without her. This is a working vacation, after all, and I'll be at the conference most of the time."

The mention of her name stopped Terri in her tracks. By the time she came to her senses, the Swedish ivy was already drowning. Her heart had stopped for a beat or two, leaving a silence so complete, she was sure she heard the poor plant crying out for help, although it might have been her own mind screaming in protest. *Maybe putting that call through wasn't such a good idea after all...*

Shuddering as a sudden chill struck her to the bone, Terri moved on to the ficus. It waved its waxy leaves as though warning her to keep quiet so it could also hear what the boss was saying. Terri gave it a wink, silently assuring it that she wasn't about to open her mouth. Not yet, anyway.

"I know I don't usually take her with me," Jacqueline went on, "but she'll have a fabulous time, and she deserves a much better vacation than she can afford herself. I couldn't possibly break my promise to her now!"

None of these statements sounded like anything Jacqueline had ever said to Terri before—not in all the five years she'd been Jacqueline's assistant. Terri studied her briefly, trying to determine if the tall blonde had been replaced by a pod-person.

"Yes, the suite is big enough for all three of us," Jacqueline admitted—though a bit grudgingly in Terri's opinion. "It has two bedrooms and a fabulous view of the ocean. You *know* how claustrophobic I get in a tiny little space. "

Ben might not have known it, but Terri did. At least, that was what Jacqueline had always told her.

"Yes, and she can keep you company while I'm at the conference." To Terri's dismay, Jacqueline seemed to be warming up to the scheme. "She won't have *that* much work to do. Like I said, I intended for her to have a nice vacation while we're there."

This time, Terri's heart not only stopped, her respiratory drive went on hiatus. A few more statements like that and she'd be dead. Moving on to the prayer plant, she caressed the graceful, striped leaves as she silently begged it to say a prayer for her.

"Oh, it'll be so much fun. What a lovely idea!" Terri could hear the note of panic underlying the honeyed insincerity in Jacqueline's voice, something Ben would be bound to notice unless they had a really lousy connection. Then again, he might not have talked to her enough during their ten-year marriage to be able to identify her inflections. Marriages between two professionals didn't always make for the best communication, and Jacqueline had been actively avoiding Ben for at least as long as Terri had known her.

She'd never had one good word to say about him. The only possible explanation Terri had ever been able to come up with for their marriage was that Jacqueline must've thought being married was good for her image. There seemed to be no other reason for it because she certainly didn't want to have children and spent as little time with Ben as possible. The child issue had been a serious bone of contention between them recently, and with Jacqueline's biological clock winding down, Terri suspected that Ben had finally reached the point of issuing an ultimatum.

Terri had given up trying to understand their relationship. Perhaps being married to a notable architect looked good on a resume, although Terri couldn't imagine that Jacqueline would need a "trophy" husband. She was enough of a hot-shot advertising executive without him.

Jacqueline's only apparent use for her husband was to avoid sexual involvements with anyone else—male or female. Terri thought it fortunate that Jacqueline had never had any children and shuddered to think just how messed up they would have been. Perhaps her husband felt that he could fill the roles of both mother and father, but Terri wouldn't even have wanted her genes.

"Well, then, goodbye, sweetheart," Jacqueline said sweetly. She had control of herself now. Even her smile looked genuine. "I'll see you on the beach, and don't forget your swimming trunks!"

Switching off the phone, she tossed it onto her desk. Her smile was gone, along with her lilting tone. "Terri, you need a plane ticket to Myrtle Beach, and you need it now."

"Departure date?"

"Now," she replied. "Today. Tomorrow morning at the latest. I'm leaving tomorrow afternoon at four, and I want you there ahead of me, in the hotel room and ready to work."

"No problem," Terri said briskly.

So much for one blissful week of doing absolutely nothing for anyone but herself. No walks in the park, no shopping, no sci-fi movie marathons. Actually, it didn't matter what Terri did, as long as she wasn't at Jacqueline's beck and call.

The plane ticket would pose no problem, although packing up and getting to the airport before noon the next day might be tricky. A flight that same day would be even worse because with no hotel reservation for the night, she'd wind up sleeping on the plane or at the airport. But, of course, that was Terri's concern, not Jacqueline's.

With a barely audible sigh, she returned to her desk and logged onto her computer, thinking she might get lucky and not find a flight. The odds were in her favor, but something told her that her evil genie was working overtime.

Last time I listen to him…

ℰℛ

Ben hung up the phone knowing exactly how Jackie felt about him butting into her conference and, therefore, her life. She was pissed. It never showed, of course. None of his wife's emotions ever did—not the genuine ones anyway—but he knew not to be fooled. Jackie had been putting him off for so long he'd come to expect it and he knew the signs. He wasn't even sure he loved her anymore, but marriage meant something to him. And so did his life. He was sick and tired of waiting for it to begin.

Part of him was wishing this would finish it, once and for all, but the voice of his conscience made him stick it out, no matter how Jackie felt, even if other people were laughing at him. No one had ever laughed openly—in fact, most men were envious of him—but that was only because Ben didn't share his marital problems with anyone. They were private, inviolate, and he saw no reason to make them food for common gossip. Outwardly, he was happily married, and if he didn't see his wife every day, well, that was simply the byproduct of a marriage between two professionals who were both bent on establishing their careers.

The trouble was, both of their careers were about as established as they were ever going to get. Jackie had never given any indication that she'd changed her mind about having a family, nor did she show any signs of slacking off in her relentless drive to the top. She was still determined to start her own advertising agency before she hit the age of forty, and at thirty-six, she was getting damned close.

Still, her biological clock was ticking, and Ben had no desire to spend his retirement watching his kids graduate high school. He was giving it one last ditch effort and then, come hell or high water, he was calling it quits. It might take him a couple of years to find a woman who actually wanted children, but there were bound to be a few of them out there somewhere.

Running a hand through his hair, he sighed deeply. "Guess I'd better get packing."

ഇരു

As luck would have it, Terri had managed to get a six-thirty flight out of LaGuardia the next morning. Unfortunately, so had *he*.

Terri had never seen Ben in person, but she'd seen his picture sitting on Jacqueline's desk often enough that she recognized him immediately. He'd aged a bit since that photograph was taken—it had been taken at their wedding—but a man that striking was hard to miss.

Jacqueline had referred to Ben as her ugly husband a million times, but Terri didn't agree. True, he wasn't classically handsome, but he certainly wasn't ugly, and he *did* stand out in a crowd. Over six feet tall and well-built with strong features and curly brown hair, Ben would have gotten Terri's attention even if he'd been a total stranger, which was unusual for her. Ordinarily, she never gave men a second look.

Having followed him through the security checks and then on to the gate area, she was able to observe him without being noticed. She'd always considered herself to be somewhat invisible and doubted he even saw her. Of course, the fact that he was clearly mesmerized by a pair of small children might have had something to do with his lack of awareness.

The boy was about three years old, blond with expressive eyes and an impish smile. The girl was even younger, a shy, ethereal blonde with a complexion like that of a china doll. Despite her reticence, she seemed to find Ben fascinating. She hid behind her mother and frequently peered around her to catch a glimpse of him before retreating once more to safety.

Having established that Ben was a trustworthy sort after he'd retrieved an errant ball for him, the boy showed him his treasured helicopter and spent the next several minutes explaining what each part of it was designed to do. Ben seemed genuinely amused, barely suppressing a smile before finally laughing out loud at something the boy said. He glanced up briefly, and his eyes met Terri's, the full impact of his captivating grin triggering an immediate pang in the vicinity of her heart.

Closing her eyes, Terri bit her lip to avoid crying out, not only in pain, but in frustration. For, like a curse that had been following her around for years just waiting for the most inopportune moment to strike, Cupid's nasty little arrow had found her at last.

And he was her boss's husband, the man she had to entertain while Jacqueline went to her conference. Staying in the same hotel with him. In the same two-bedroom oceanfront condo.

Along with the boss from hell.

Holy shit.

Chapter 2

Terri had never been tempted by a man in her life. She didn't necessarily dislike men; she just didn't see that they were anything to get excited about. Whenever her girlfriends drooled, she'd remained unmoved—and overlooked. Unlike so many women Terri knew.

Her friend Constance was a perfect example. Married fairly young and recently divorced, Constance had since had several boyfriends who were, for the most part, worthless—at least one of them having wound up in jail. She'd finally found a nice man who even had a good job, but she'd come in one morning the week before looking completely exhausted. Later, by the coffee pot, which she normally avoided, she told Terri the reason. People were forever telling her the strangest things. Being a woman of few words always encouraged others to spill their guts in her direction—whether she was truly interested or not—and this time was no different. She'd merely appeared curious at the unfamiliar sight of Constance with a coffee mug in her hand...

"I was at a *family* party," Constance wailed. "I ran into an old friend who was on leave from Iraq. I'd never dated him, never had sex with him, but I was drunk. He took me home with him, and I was going to sleep on the couch, but—"

"Don't you have a boyfriend?" Terri inquired innocently.

"Well, yeah," she muttered. "But it was late and I was too drunk to drive, so he took me home. Then he asked me if I'd seen the sign above his door."

"Sign?"

"Yeah, the one that said that anyone entering after midnight had to stay until morning—"

"And?"

"And had to be naked by two."

How clever. "So, I take it you were up all night, then."

She nodded grimly. "He fucked me for six and a half hours. He wore me out! We did *everything.* Twice! I had to ask him to stop a couple of times. I couldn't take any more. Every bone in my body hurts. I think he must have taken Viagra."

"And did he?"

"He swore he didn't. He'd just been saving it up for a while, I guess."

Terri had nodded, smiled, and mentally told Constance she was a slut. She didn't say it out loud, of course, although Constance probably would have agreed. Still, it served as a point of comparison, for here was a woman, just a few years younger— prettier, perhaps, and with a spectacular figure—but Terri had never been with a man for six and a half minutes, let alone six and a half hours. Somehow, it seemed ever-so-slightly unfair…

Just as unfair as things seemed now. Here was Ben, whom Jacqueline didn't love, rarely saw, yet seemed unlikely to divorce— and whom Terri would have taken in a heartbeat, purely on the basis of his smile.

Terri closed her eyes on the scene before her, wondering if anyone else in the entire world realized what had happened. There was no outward change, but inside, she'd gone numb from the shock. Light-headed and dizzy, she wondered how she would survive the flight—something she didn't enjoy even on a good day.

Why now? And why him? Terri knew she was different from other women and was at a loss to explain why she'd been such a late bloomer. There'd been no trauma in her life, no event that marked her as unlikely to ever fall in love. Boys had never seemed interested in her, nor had she encouraged them to be. Her mind had simply been on other matters. Until now.

She could have gone right on sitting there with her eyes closed in an effort to blot him out of her mind and stop her head from swimming, if only her phone hadn't been ringing. Dear, sweet Jacqueline was calling to make sure Terri was on time for her flight.

"Are you there yet?" Jacqueline asked briskly.

"Yes." *And I've already fallen in love with your husband. Am I fired? Please? Pretty please?*

"You *do* know what he looks like, don't you?" Terri could picture Jacqueline's moue of distaste. "I'm sure you must have seen his photograph. Tall, homely, big ears?"

Poor Ben. Terri had listened to Jacqueline bad-mouthing him for years and had always figured that a good bit of that criticism was undeserved. Now she knew that the disparaging remarks about his appearance were completely unfounded, for she'd never seen a more appealing man in her life. Jacqueline obviously needed to see an optometrist. It was on the tip of Terri's tongue to ask if she should set up an appointment, but, as usual, she didn't say what she was thinking. "Yes."

"Well, I think he's on an early flight. Is he there by any chance?"

"Yes, he is."

"Great!" Her enthusiasm made Terri want to strangle her. "Introduce yourself and get to know him a little bit. Go ahead and rent a car. I'll get one myself. That way the two of you won't have to be stuck at the hotel while I'm at the conference."

Which meant that if Terri went anywhere, it would have to be with Ben—unless she walked or took a cab. "I don't drive."

"Oh." Jacqueline paused for a moment. "Well, Ben can, so that won't be a problem. Just be your usual efficient self and keep him under control until I get there. Remember, you're there to keep him from getting ideas. He's been badgering me to have a baby again, and I'm counting on you to keep things from getting too personal between us."

Terri couldn't begin to imagine how she was supposed to do that unless she and Jacqueline shared a room. Aside from the fact that hell would have to freeze over first, how on earth would they explain it? Terri's heart skipped a beat as another thought occurred to her.

No. She can't possibly mean I'm supposed to do that…

"Terri, are you still there?"

"Yeah," Terri replied. "I'm here."

"Listen, just get me through this and I'll give you a big bonus and another week of paid vacation. Anywhere you want to go." The *or else* was implied, but Terri heard it loud and clear.

"No problem." Although it was her standard response, Terri really didn't mean it this time. How long would all this take? Jacqueline was somewhere in her late thirties. Did Terri have to keep her husband away from her until menopause? Or would Ben finally give up and divorce her at some point? He wasn't getting any younger, either—a bit older than Jacqueline, which would put him at somewhere around forty. Assessing him briefly, Terri didn't think he looked anywhere near that old—especially when he smiled. Her eyes softened as she took in his boyish grin. She truly felt bad for him. Who could blame a man for wanting to have children? It was rather sweet of him, really. But why didn't he simply divorce Jacqueline and be done with it? After all, a man like that would have no trouble finding someone else.

The obvious reason presented itself with astonishing swiftness. He was in love with Jacqueline. Terri shuddered with revulsion. She couldn't imagine many fates worse than being in love with a woman like Jacqueline Tremaine. *Manipulative, cunning, self-serving…* Terri's list could have gone on, but she was already feeling depressed and didn't see the point.

God help the man who really loves you. Terri had never fully understood Rhett Butler's words to Scarlet O'Hara—until now. She felt genuinely sorry for Ben. She didn't have to know him to know that he deserved better.

The kindest thing Terri could have done would be to simply walk over and tell him to forget it and go home. She didn't. No, after reassuring Jacqueline that she would do her best, Terri said goodbye, got to her feet, pasted on a smile, and approached Ben with a brisk efficiency intended to cover any other feelings she might have.

As Ben's curious gaze swept her from head to toe, Terri's step and smile both faltered. She knew what he was *seeing*—a rather plain, slightly chubby woman with ordinary features, shoulder-length brown hair, and blue eyes which were difficult to see through her rather thick-lensed glasses—but what was he *thinking?*

Whatever it was, she knew it couldn't be good, but his expression gave nothing away. "You must be Terri," he said, holding out a hand. "Jackie said we might be on the same flight. Mind telling me how she talked you into doing this?"

She shrugged. "Part of the job."

Her remark didn't seem to surprise him, proving he knew a little something about the woman he'd married. He took her hand in a warm, firm grasp. "Did she at least pay for your plane ticket?"

"Yes." Terri was astonished that she was able to say even that much, because not only was he holding her hand, he was smiling at her in a most devastating manner. Tousled, sandy curls tumbled over his forehead, and his twinkling green eyes captured her gaze completely. All she could think of was that she should call Jacqueline back and resign, or trade in her ticket and leave the country—anything other than blithely following her orders.

"Well, that was decent of her," he said, smoothly filling in the silence that followed Terri's reply. "It's bad enough making you work during your vacation."

Her response was automatic. "I don't mind."

He quirked a skeptical eyebrow, but let it pass. "Just what sort of work will you be doing?"

"Correspondence." Which was what she normally did, anyway. "And planning her schedule at the conference."

Terri felt an immediate sense of loss as he released her hand. "She could have done that herself."

She didn't comment, but inwardly agreed.

"Or maybe she thought you needed to get out of the city for a while."

She choked back a derisive snort. "Possibly."

He grinned. "The Big Apple been getting you down?"

"Not really."

Although he nodded, he didn't seem convinced, which came as no surprise to Terri. He probably knew exactly why she was there, and the fact that she and Jacqueline weren't on the same flight smacked of a last-minute scramble. Terri wasn't holding up well under interrogation and would be grateful when he finally stopped asking questions she couldn't answer.

She knew that he and her boss rarely vacationed—or did anything else—together. To the best of her knowledge, they didn't even live in the same house most of the time. Jacqueline had an upscale apartment in the city, while he claimed to prefer a quieter place in the country with a longer commute. *What a pair*...

"Well... I just thought I should introduce myself," she said lamely. "I'll be over there..." Waving a vague thumb in the direction of her seat, she walked away on a pair of legs that weren't quite as steady as usual. Of the many things she'd regretted doing—or *not* doing—in her life, this was undoubtedly going to end up being the absolute top. Sinking gratefully into her chair, she kept her eyes closed until the flight boarded.

This, however, did nothing to quiet her tumultuous brain, and thoughts buzzed through her head like angry bees. *Jacqueline doesn't want his children, but he wouldn't want me. I can't have him, but she doesn't want him. Jacqueline wants to be married, but not really*... It was enough to drive anyone crazy.

Boarding began, and Terri found her seat, which fortunately was *not* next to Ben's. Buckling her safety belt, she closed her eyes again. To divert her mind, she daydreamed about a possible terrorist hijacking attempt. She would be the lone passenger who sacrificed her life to save the others, throwing herself in harm's way to distract the terrorists while the other passengers—including Ben—acted heroically to subdue the perpetrators. The flight would reach its destination, and her lifeless body would be carried from the plane with honor.

Ben would tell the reporters what a wonderful person she'd been. It wouldn't matter that they were barely acquainted because no one ever says anything bad about the hero of a situation like that. Terri had never heard anyone say, "Yeah, the guy was a real shit-head, but he did at least one good thing in his miserable, worthless life." A horrific fate, perhaps, but infinitely preferable to the prospect of having to face Jacqueline—or her husband—ever again.

The flight seemed to last an eternity, and Terri gave up on the notion of an attendant offering her anything stronger than tea or coffee at seven in the morning. She didn't drink alcohol as a rule, but the realization that it would be much too early to check into the hotel when they arrived was about to drive her to drink. She'd have to kill the time somehow, and hoped she wouldn't be expected to do it with *him*.

Then it occurred to her that she would be killing time with Ben for the entire *week* and would be there with him every day while the bitch from hell was at her damned conference. Avoiding him now would only prolong the inevitable. She'd be stuck babysitting him no matter what she did. Maybe she could disappear every day until nightfall, reappearing just in time to somehow keep him out of Jacqueline's bed—which brought her back to the ridiculous nature of her mission. *What the hell am I supposed to do? Seduce him?*

Her sudden burst of laughter undoubtedly had the woman sitting next to her convinced she'd gone stark, raving mad. *Maybe I have.* The very idea that she could seduce *anyone*, let alone the husband of her beautiful and sophisticated boss, was preposterous. Unless he enjoyed charming mousy little women out of their pantyhose, he probably wouldn't even see her as being female. She was a drone and a worker; nothing more. Necessary, perhaps, but both sexless and insignificant.

The puzzle of how to keep them apart occupied Terri's mind for the remainder of the flight, but she came up with very little that seemed practical. She could stay up half the night working and knock on their door at an inopportune moment to ask Jacqueline about some obscure, but pertinent detail. Or she could develop a sleep-walking affliction, stumbling in on them when she heard Jacqueline protest that she couldn't do it with Terri in the next room.

Nightmares would be good. Periodic blood-curdling screams would ruin the mood for anyone but a pervert—which was about the only disparaging remark Jacqueline had never made about Ben. Then there was the possibility that the mere sight of Terri in a bathing suit might be enough to make him swear off women entirely. *One could only hope.* Of course, that meant she would actually have to go out and *buy* one…

Then she realized that Jacqueline would undoubtedly be using some form of birth control, so having sex wouldn't be the issue. What Terri had to prevent was the *discussion.* Simply being in the same room with them would do the trick during the day, but at night? She would have to share a room with one of them, but other than developing a sudden, unreasonable fear of being left alone in a hotel bedroom, she couldn't see how to explain the need for a roommate.

Then it occurred to her that she wouldn't have to *do* anything; just being there would be enough to deter him, and was probably all that Jacqueline expected of her. That much, she could do. After putting up with Jacqueline's moods and whims, how hard could it be?

With that heartening thought, Terri relaxed for the rest of the flight, and when she deplaned, it was with the attitude that she would handle this assignment as capably as everything else Jacqueline had ever asked her to do. Then she saw Ben and the same heart-stopping thing happened again. Never having felt that way about a man in her life, she had no way of knowing whether she could keep her eyes off him or not. On the other hand, if having unattractive, lovesick females fawning over him was a regular occurrence, he might not notice. He would probably pay no more attention to her than he did the others.

Unless, he *didn't* ignore them. With a sinking feeling, Terri realized that a normal, healthy male like Ben probably wouldn't be satisfied with the tiny little bit of affection he got from Jacqueline. *Of course he has affairs!* He'd have to or he'd go nuts—at least, that was what she assumed. Men were supposed to all be panting sex maniacs, although she'd seen very little evidence to back it up—unless Constance and her six-and-a-half-hour fun fest partner were typical. Somehow, she didn't think they were.

As it turned out, any attempts Terri might have made to avoid or ignore Ben would have been useless. He was waiting for her when she got off the plane, and they went together to pick up their luggage.

He talked along the way in a very friendly fashion, seeming not to notice her monosyllabic replies—or so she thought.

"You don't seem very happy about being here," he commented as Terri stood silently waiting for her suitcase to appear on the luggage carousel. "I mean, I seem to recall Jackie mentioning that you were pretty quiet as a rule, but I would have thought that on vacation you would be a little more…cheerful."

Vacation? This wasn't a *vacation.* This was playing gooseberry for the boss and her adorable husband. At least she would have that second week off when she got home; a paid vacation to anywhere she wanted to travel. *Ah, bliss…* "I don't like to fly."

"Well, cheer up, then," he said brightly. "That part's over with."

Terri replied with a nod, thinking perhaps she could use the excuse of dreading the return flight to explain her sulks from then on.

He seemed about to comment further, but she spotted her ancient suitcase and stepped forward to claim it, wishing she'd had time to buy a new one. She was a little surprised at herself for caring—her suitcase couldn't possibly matter to anyone anyway.

"So, what's next on the agenda?" He was still using that same chipper tone—the sort one would use when dealing with a grumpy child.

"Jacqueline said you should rent a car."

"Good idea," he said. "What about you?"

Apparently his graciousness didn't extend to giving her a ride to the hotel, which suited her just fine. "I'll get a cab."

"You don't want a car?"

"I don't drive."

"Oh." He sounded a bit taken aback. "Well, then…you can ride with me." He paused a moment before adding, "Why would you think you'd need to take a cab?"

Terri shrugged. "It's what I would have done if you hadn't been here." He shouldn't have been so surprised. Lots of New Yorkers didn't drive; they walked or took the subway. Besides, there were bound to be plenty of stores and restaurants near the hotel—enough to suit Terri, that is.

"I see." He frowned. "You're only getting here early so you'll have everything all set up for Jackie, aren't you?"

"Yes." What else did he think she would be there for?

Oh, yeah, to keep you away from your wife. Sorry, I forgot.

Ben heaved a sigh. "It's probably too soon to check in. What were you planning to do in the meantime?"

She shrugged. "Stay here?"

"My, how exciting," he drawled. "I thought I'd change clothes somewhere and head for the beach."

Terri couldn't blame him for his dry tone, but going to the beach meant wearing a swimsuit, and she didn't have one—something that would have seemed a little suspicious if she'd known in advance that she'd be coming along on this trip. One slip like that, and there went the extra week of paid vacation—and possibly her job.

Then inspiration struck. "I was planning to buy a new swimsuit when I got here."

"No problem. We can go shopping first. Have you had

breakfast?"

The urge to scream in frustration clogged her throat. The one thing she hadn't considered was that he would have a mind of his own. She should have known better. At that point, she gave up, deciding to tell the truth whenever possible. "No."

"Me, either. Okay then, we rent a car, have breakfast somewhere, buy you a swimsuit, and *then* go to the beach."

By that time, they could check into the hotel and bypass the beach altogether. Or, she could *really* irritate him by spending hours trying to find just the right bit of spandex to cover her ass adequately. Trying to look a bit more enthusiastic than she'd been before, she picked up her suitcase and they set off.

Chapter 3

The very last thing Ben had expected when he called Jackie was to end up squiring her assistant around Myrtle Beach, although in all honesty, he probably should have. Every time he tried a new tactic, he eventually found himself either walking away or hanging up the phone realizing she'd done it to him again.

Jackie might've taken a casual view of their marriage, but Ben hadn't. Despite her apparent dislike of anything sexual—something he wished he'd known before he'd had the misfortune to marry her—he'd stuck it out and never cheated. More and more, his marriage seemed to be in name only, simply because Jackie was too damn good at putting him off and making it seem reasonable.

And now he was stuck with her assistant. Not that he minded, really. He only wished he knew her a little better. Ben had never actually met Terri until she'd walked up to him at the airport, and all he'd ever heard about her was that she was a damn fine worker. She'd have to be to keep Jackie in line. In fact, she was just about the only person Jackie ever had a good word for. But she was an odd little duck, and so very different from Jackie, who had an opinion about everything. The best he could tell, Terri never said a word unless spoken to and sometimes didn't even answer direct questions. It was unnerving, but it was also kind of nice to be with a woman who let him take the lead—something impossible to do with Jackie.

Which was strange because anyone who'd been Jackie's assistant for as long as she had was bound to be capable of handling almost anything. Still, Terri *was* on vacation, so it paid to be polite, and he made a point of consulting her on the more pertinent points. She apparently had no preference when it came to the make, model, or color of a rental car. After renting a sporty little red car, he stowed her battered suitcase in the trunk. A glance in her direction revealed a furrowed brow and lips pressed into a thin line.

"So, where do you want to go for breakfast?"

If he'd been hoping for a smile, he didn't get one. "Surprise me."

Ben couldn't help but laugh. "Somehow, I don't think surprising you would be as easy as it sounds."

All he got for his attempt at humor was a blank stare.

"Sorry," Ben muttered. "I guess it's still too early in the morning."

Too early for much of anything, it seemed, including communication of any form because if her puzzled expression was anything to go by, he might has well have been speaking Japanese. With a shrug, he walked around to the passenger side and opened the door. Terri stood and stared at him as though he'd lost his mind.

With a gesture that was more abrupt than necessary, he said, "Hop in."

She shook her head as though she still didn't understand a word he was saying but she did get in the car. Ben slammed the door and then got in on the other side. He hesitated before starting the engine, wondering if it was worth trying to clear the air between them or not. He'd put the car in reverse and had begun backing out of the parking space, when he decided it was. Stomping on the brake, he turned toward her. "Am I making you nervous?"

"No," she replied.

"You're obviously upset about something. You didn't plan on me being here, did you?"

"No."

Which wasn't surprising. He'd come up with this idea himself and should've known how it would go. His irritation was probably quite evident, but at the moment, he really didn't care. A man ought to be able to take a vacation with his wife without it seeming like such an odd occurrence. And he ought to be able to do it without having that wife's assistant along for the ride. Snatching a map from the dashboard, he tossed it in her lap and continued backing the car. "Here, you can navigate."

She opened the map and stared at it with even more confusion. "Where are we?"

Ben rolled his eyes. "The *airport?*" Already irritated, he was rapidly losing what little patience he had left. "Are you always this stupid?"

He immediately regretted his outburst when he noticed that she was fighting back tears.

"No," she replied in a small voice. "I'm not feeling very well and looking at this map is making it worse." She closed her eyes as her head fell back against the headrest. A tear squeezed past her lashes to slide down her cheek as she let out a deep, shuddering sigh.

"Sorry. I shouldn't have said that. I'm a little on edge myself this morning." He stopped, shaking his head. "Never mind. I'll figure it out."

Terri spent the next several minutes turned away from him, gazing fixedly out the window, remaining silent even as they left the airport grounds and drove out to the main road. After passing a large shopping mall on the right, he turned north on Highway 17. She still hadn't said a word.

The silence between them was so complete that when he finally spoke again, she jumped as though he'd slapped her. "Do you know the address of the hotel?"

She kept right on staring out the window, and when she spoke, her tone was flat and colorless. "It's on North Ocean Boulevard, which should run parallel to this road, a few blocks to the east."

No, she wasn't stupid. She couldn't have been, or Jackie wouldn't have put up with her all these years. He felt like apologizing all over again, then decided he might do better to keep his mouth shut. Turning right at the next intersection, he drove three or four blocks before pulling into the parking lot of a decent-looking restaurant. She practically jumped out of the car the moment he put it in park.

Ben was already kicking himself for being so rude. Whatever his problems were with Jackie, Terri wasn't the cause. He had no right to take it out on her. Hurrying after her, he caught her by the arm just before she made it to the door and pulled her around to face him. "Hey, what do you say we start over?" With a sheepish smile, he let go of her arm and held out his hand. "Charles Benjamin Tremaine. And you are…?"

Ben half expected her to slap his hand away, but she didn't, nor did she give him the typical perfunctory handshake. Instead, she laid her small, warm hand in his grasp. Not firm, not in control, but trembling. He'd been a total jerk to upset her like that. She wasn't anything like Jackie—wasn't nearly as tough. The warmth of her hand proved that much.

"Terrington Elizabeth Marshall," she said stiffly.

He raised his gaze from Terri's hand to her face just in time to see her wince as though he'd squeezed too hard. Obviously starting over hadn't helped much. Releasing her hand, he gave her a brief nod and opened the door to the restaurant, motioning for her to enter. He followed in her wake, thinking that they probably looked like a married couple who'd been arguing over where they would be having breakfast since sunup. Going shopping with her would be interesting, to say the least.

Breakfast was a fairly quiet event; they exchanged perhaps a dozen words between them, both having more to say to the waitress than they did to each other. Ben suspected there was something else going on with her—something that perhaps had nothing to do with him or even Jackie. Whatever it was, it was affecting not only her mood, but her appetite. His own breakfast tasted fine, so he doubted his choice of restaurants was the cause, but from the way she picked at her food, she was bound to be a wraith by the end of the week.

By his second cup of coffee, Ben felt much better and wished Terri could have felt the same, but her mood hadn't improved. She continued to stare at her plate, pushing her omelet around with the same morose expression. Making himself a solemn promise not to snap at her again, he did his best to smile and sound cheerful about spending the rest of the day with her. "Are you ready to go find that perfect bathing suit?"

She nodded. "Sure."

It was on the tip of his tongue to tell her to curb her enthusiasm, but he remembered his promise, consoling himself with the fact that she wasn't giving him the silent treatment—at least, not totally.

Finding a place to buy a swimsuit was no problem since there was a store selling beach gear on just about every corner. Terri seemed to have no more preference for this than she'd had for breakfast, so he chose a shop at random. Once inside, he did his best to seem attentive and helpful, but the way she stood between him and whatever rack of swimwear she was perusing made him wonder if she wasn't wishing he'd waited in the car—which he might have done if it hadn't been so damned hot. As it was, he saw no need to get roasted alive when there was an air-conditioned store on hand.

After watching her choose a few modest one-piece suits to try on, she was in the dressing room when Ben's gaze landed on a bikini and he was seized with a sudden urge to see her in it. It was certainly prettier—and sexier—than anything else she'd selected. Perhaps it would be just the thing to improve her mood. *Maybe she just needs a little push.* Figuring he had nothing to lose, he snatched up one in the same size as the suits she'd picked out and knocked on the dressing room door.

Terri had already rejected the first suit she'd tried on. It made her look even fatter than she thought she was, if that was possible. Apparently the suit that would make her appear twenty pounds lighter didn't exist.

Clad only in her panties, she was reaching for the next suit with about as much enthusiasm as she would've felt for a boa constrictor when Ben rapped on the door.

"Here, try this one," he said, flipping a purple and white

flowered bikini over the door.

If the other suit was a boa constrictor, this one was definitely a cobra. Terri stared at it just waiting for it to strike. *Oh, wow... Low blow...* He had to have known she couldn't possibly fit into the damned thing; he was just trying to make her feel bad. He'd already accused her of being stupid, which she was most definitely *not*. Quiet, perhaps, but certainly not stupid. Then she spotted the tag. Apparently he'd been paying attention, despite her efforts to hide the fact that she had been looking at the size sixteens.

The hanger was still hooked on his finger, and when she didn't respond, he jiggled it up and down. "What's the matter? Don't you think it's pretty?"

Maybe. On anybody but me. It looked just fine on the hanger, too, but Terri wasn't about to put it on. No possible way.

"Come on, now," he cajoled. "Just try it. You'll look great."

Already suspecting that after his initial irritation he'd been trying to kill her with kindness, he now appeared to be making a valiant attempt at trying to win her over with flattery—although why he felt the need to do so was a mystery. What did her mood matter to him anyway? On the other hand, if his desire was to embarrass her to death, this would be just the thing because there wasn't a snowball's chance in hell that something that skimpy would look good on her. Not in this lifetime.

"No," she said firmly.

"Terri," he said with a hint of warning in his voice. "Put it on, or I'm leaving here without you."

If embarrassment was his ulterior motive, he obviously wasn't above making threats to achieve it. Then she realized why. It was his revenge for her being there to come between him and his wife. The worst part of it was, she probably deserved it for agreeing to participate in this farce to begin with. It didn't matter if he ever realized she knew precisely why she was there because he was bound to figure it out eventually. And once he did, she would probably wind up unemployed in addition to whatever torment he might dish out. Her anger flaring, she snatched the hanger from his finger, hoping she might get lucky and yank off his fingernail in the process.

Snarling when she heard him chuckling rather than bellowing out in pain, she ripped it off the hanger. She'd never had on a bikini in her life and didn't even wear bikini underwear. *Yet another first for this trip.* Pulling the neck strap over her head, she hooked the back before stepping angrily into the bottom half and stuffing her panties down below the waistband. Not even bothering to glance at the mirror, she yanked open the door for about a half a second, and then slammed it shut again.

Or tried to. Ben was too quick for her, catching the edge of the door and prying it open with his fingers.

Terri caught a brief glimpse of an expression she'd never before seen on the face of anyone who happened to be looking in her direction.

His jaw dropped. *"Wow."*

Terri couldn't decide whether to kill him or throw her arms around him and kiss his lips off. *Those full, sensuous lips...*

A quick mental slap brought her back to reality. Men's lips were neither full, nor sensuous. Particularly the lips of her boss's husband. Then she remembered the whole Cupid thing. That would explain it. Still, she *did* like that look in his eyes...

A look that was still there. Licking his lower lip, he said, "You're buying that one, aren't you? Because if you don't, I will."

Terri knew that Jacqueline would have a fit if she let Ben buy her anything, especially a bikini, and Terri didn't particularly care for the idea herself. It was too... personal. Wearing it made her feel almost naked, and the way Ben's gaze was riveted to her chest made her nipples tingle. Heat flooded her core in a way she'd never experienced. *I should've stayed home.*

She shook her head. "I don't think so. I'm sure I look like a blimp in this thing."

"No, you don't." His voice sounded rough. "You look..." He

stopped there, either unable to find the right word or unwilling to say it. He swallowed with apparent difficulty. "Turn around."

Terri frowned, but did as he asked.

Ben let out a groan. "Oh, God."

"What?" Obviously the bikini hadn't done anything for the size of her butt, which must've looked enormous. "If it looks *that* bad, I don't want it."

"It doesn't look bad, and you need to buy it. Trust me."

Terri glanced over her shoulder, catching another glimpse of Ben's open-mouthed stare, only this time his eyes weren't on her chest. "You're sure?"

"Absolutely. Buy it."

There was no point in starting another argument, and Ben had probably had his fill of shopping. "Well, okay. If you say so." Not waiting for any further comments, she closed the door behind her and got dressed.

When she came out, Ben was waiting for her with a beach towel and a lacy cover-up, both as purple as the bikini. "You need these, too."

"Oh, really?" He was being awfully free with her money. Then again, she had nothing better to spend it on at the moment.

"Yes, really."

Terri had never had anyone tell her what she needed to buy before and wasn't quite sure how to take it. "You're sure I don't need anything else? What about sandals and sunscreen? Or a beach bag?"

"Those, too."

Obviously sarcasm was lost on him. Terri reminded herself that if they took long enough, their rooms would be ready and going to the beach would be unnecessary. "Sure. Whatever you think best."

Unfortunately, she hadn't figured on Ben being such an efficient shopper. Within fifteen minutes, he had her completely outfitted and out of the shop.

Damn.

Chapter 4

Ben found the hotel without any difficulty, but the desk clerk very politely informed them that their rooms wouldn't be ready until the afternoon. Unable to think of any excuses not to, Terri changed into her bikini in the restroom of the main lobby. Donning the flimsy cover-up and sandals, she stuffed her clothes into her new beach bag and went out.

The vast expanse of sparkling ocean and sandy beach that comprised the Grand Strand was breathtaking, but Ben in swimming trunks nearly did her in. Tall, lean, and broad-shouldered, he reminded her of a young Charlton Heston—all he needed was a chariot and a team of horses to complete the picture. Or a loincloth. Speedos would've been a nice touch too.

The surliness of the morning was completely gone. Ben was the perfect beach companion, perfectly willing to put sunscreen on her back. Terri sucked in a ragged breath as his hot hands spread the creamy lotion on her skin. She'd never had an orgasm, but suspected that Ben could elicit that response with nothing more than a back rub.

Never much of a swimmer, Terri had to be lured into the sea. But Ben was like a Siren in male form. Laughing, smiling, filled with charmingly boyish enthusiasm, he was there to catch her when the waves slammed into her, making her squeal with laughter. He built a sand castle as precise as any architect would, but since sand wasn't his normal medium, it collapsed on itself before ever being hit by a wave. Joined by a bunch of kids, he demolished it with equal zest.

For a few short, but idyllic hours, she got a taste of what it would be like to enjoy vacationing with a husband or a boyfriend. She now knew what she'd been missing all her life—and would continue to miss unless someone else came along, because *he* was already married. She would give herself that brief space of time to pretend and then it would be over. Jacqueline would arrive and things would change. Terri refused to let her boss catch her mooning over her husband. She would go back to being her usual invisible self and that would be the end of it. Cupid could just go shoot himself in the foot.

Of course, he'd also have to shoot her eyes out because after seeing Ben on the beach in a pair of swimming trunks she was beginning to understand why women drooled. Then he went and made matters worse—much, *much* worse.

"Hey, would you put some of that on me?" he asked as she coated her arm with Coppertone. "I'd hate to get burnt to a crisp on the first day. Talk about something that would ruin your vacation."

Groaning inwardly, she nodded as he crawled over to sit in front of her on her towel, insinuating his body between her outstretched legs. Adding a dollop of lotion to her hands, she rubbed her palms together before reaching up to touch his back. He was so close she could have leaned forward and laid her head on him. She probably took longer over the task than was strictly necessary, but she simply couldn't help herself. Delighting in the feel of his hot, smooth skin beneath her hands, she kept on until mere application became a massage, and then later, a caress. The fact that he sighed with pleasure from time to time should have been a deterrent, but it wasn't. It was an incentive.

A group of laughing children scurried past, kicking up sand in their wake, distracting her from her task and bringing her back to reality. With a start, Terri realized that he'd moved back farther, pressing against her to the point that his hips were now touching her inner thighs. She felt it then, and though she'd never felt it before, she knew it for exactly what it was.

Desire.

Need.

Lust.

The time had come to put a stop to this. Quickly. "There you go," she said, giving him a brisk pat on the shoulder.

As she began to rise, he stopped her. "Hold on, Terri. You probably could stand a little more sunscreen too."

The first time he'd touched her had been bad enough. Now, she sat there, helpless to prevent it, as Ben got up on his hands and knees and crawled around behind her, sitting, just as she had done, with her hips between his legs. However, unlike Terri, Ben wasn't content with simply getting close enough to reach her back. Oh, no. He snuggled up against her hips and thighs before his warm, strong hands melted into her shoulders. She was pretty sure she even felt his...

Oh, my God!

She'd inadvertently sent him a message which he'd received loud and clear, and he was delivering his reply—personally.

What was going on? He loved Jacqueline, didn't he? He was even badgering her to have children, which made this behavior completely nonsensical. He'd taken Terri to breakfast, stuffed her into a purple bikini, and now seemed intent on turning her into a home wrecker. She was supposed to be playing gooseberry, not the "other woman."

Terri gave him just long enough to do an adequate job, and then got up abruptly and headed for the water. She was waist deep in the ocean before she remembered something. God knew he didn't get much in the way of love and affection from Jacqueline. He probably was accustomed to having little affairs. Perhaps he thought that was what she was there for...

Oh, surely not. Jacqueline wouldn't have brought her along for something like *that.* Not without telling her...or would she? Terri knew Jacqueline rarely spent much time with Ben—and when she spoke of him at all, it was never with affection—but she'd certainly never asked Terri to find him a woman. Then again, perhaps she'd never needed to. Maybe he usually supplied his own.

This was just too weird. These people simply weren't normal. Why would each of them keep their previous home after they were married? Jacqueline had lived in her posh Manhattan apartment for at least as long as Terri had known her. Probably longer. Ben's house was supposed to have been his parent's home at one time, and she could understand why he'd be reluctant to give it up, particularly if he wanted a family. Perhaps their living apart *did* make some sense, but not a whole lot.

She was probably overreacting. Never having been in close contact with a man before, she was completely out of her element. Constance would have behaved very differently. In Terri's place, she would have flirted outrageously with Ben and slept with him before the week was out.

But did married men really *do* things like that? Married men who wanted to stay married, that is? It was possible that he didn't love Jacqueline and was trying to goad her into a divorce. If she'd never agreed to it before, that could be the reason he was doing this now. But a person couldn't *make* you stay married to them, could they? Movie stars filed for divorce all the time, and their spouses weren't always keen on the idea. He could do that if Jacqueline refused, of course, but even so, Terri simply didn't get it.

She stood amid the waves, letting them rock her with their steady rhythm. She hadn't done anything so bad. Ben had been a bit short with her earlier, and now he was trying to make it up to her by being attentive and friendly. She was the one who was acting weird, not him. She might've taken an arrow through the heart that morning, but Ben didn't know anything about that. There was nothing odd going on—it was only that her inexperience was showing. All she needed to do was to chill out.

As she waded back to the shore, she spotted Ben lying on his towel in the sand. She had to get fairly close before she could see him clearly since she'd taken her glasses off when they'd arrived at the beach, but she still had a moment or two to observe him before he realized she was there. There was nothing so very special about him, really. She'd seen lots of men who were more handsome, several of whom she saw on a daily basis. Constance had slept with most of the attractive guys and refused to sleep with the homely ones. She'd also told Terri a few things about their anatomy that they might not have wanted to become common knowledge.

Holding up an index finger one morning, Constance had exclaimed with a giggle, "His dick is only that long!" Roger surely wouldn't have wanted anyone to know that little tidbit, and besides, he couldn't help it if he was small. A penis wasn't something he could build up like his biceps. However, Terri had considered bringing this unfortunate characteristic up a time or two because Roger could be a real shithead when the spirit moved him. The odd thing was that Constance had spent the night with him more than once, small cock or not.

Sitting down on her towel, Terri put her glasses back on to gaze out at the ocean. Ben appeared to be asleep, and she subsequently found herself doing something she'd never done before. Boy watching.

Most were quite young, but some looked at least old enough to drive, and a good many were old enough to drink legally in any state. Swaggering down the beach in their baggy shorts, what was between their waist and knees was left to the imagination, but little else was. Tanned, burned, thin, fat, white, black, and everything in between, they came in all shapes, colors, and sizes. Some studiously ignored the women, while others were quite obviously there for the sole purpose of being seen and admired.

A quick glance at Ben reassured Terri that he hadn't caught her at her new hobby. And even if he had, she might have simply been looking at the sea. After all, it was big enough to attract anyone's attention.

Keeping her expression carefully neutral—which it was most of the time anyway—and displaying no interest beyond the casual, she sat and waited for more men to wander by. After a moment or two, a pair of them walked past, one tall and dark, while the other was shorter and more compact with curly brown hair. They couldn't have been much more than twenty or so, both very cute and nicely built. A whole pack ran by not long after that, and, realizing that she was enjoying herself just a bit, she wondered why she hadn't tried this years ago. This was an easy question to answer since, generally speaking, she didn't hang out at the beach. But the fact remained that she could have done it anywhere—in a store, on the street—not as much skin, perhaps, but *still*... And, who knew? Maybe that Cupid's arrow thing had been a fluke. Or maybe it could strike twice…

Ben stirred beside her. "You should turn over," Terri advised. "I'm sure that side's done by now."

He rolled over like an obedient dog. "How about some more lotion?"

"I believe you can handle the front side," she replied, unperturbed.

"But I like it better when you do it," he said with a sigh. "You've got awfully good hands."

After giving him an admonitory glance, she returned her gaze to the sea. "You know, you're mighty chummy for a man I just met this morning."

"Maybe. It's just that I've heard Jackie mention you off and on for a long time. I feel like I've known you forever."

Terri simply nodded in reply, but wondered what Jacqueline had said about her. Then she remembered all the cutting remarks Jacqueline had made about Ben over the years and decided she really didn't want to know. Terri had only just met him and had already decided that Jacqueline's criticism of him had been rather harsh. So far, she liked him. But it was hard to tell whether it was that Cupid thing, or if she would've liked him anyway.

Upon further reflection she decided that she probably would have. They'd gotten off to a rocky start, but Ben wasn't such a bad guy, really. He'd even said he liked the way she looked in a bikini, which was something she'd never heard from anyone before. Not that there'd ever been an opportunity…

That same pair of boys walked by again, and Terri caught the shorter one's eye. *Oh, what the hell…* She kept on watching, turning her head and allowing her gaze to follow him. Staring back over his shoulder, he nudged his companion, who also turned to look. A moment or two later he stumbled as, not watching where he was going, he put a foot in a hole some kid had dug in the sand.

Suppressing a smile, Terri glanced away and picked up the bottle of Coppertone. Her evil genie then gave her a nudge, causing her to squirt Ben right in the middle of his chest.

He let out a yelp. "What did I ever do to deserve that?"

"You made me cry," she reminded him. "Paybacks are hell."

"Well, I didn't *mean* to make you cry," he said, rubbing the lotion over his chest. "And I believe I apologized, I just—well, if I've heard about you from Jackie, you're bound to have heard about me."

"So?"

"You've got to know that things aren't what you'd call perfect between us."

"It's none of my business."

"Maybe so, but you know how she is. She can be very nice to your face, and then turn around and stab you in the back."

So, she'd said some pretty nasty things about me, had she? I figured as much. "I don't believe we should be having this conversation."

"But you're a nice girl. If she was planning something dastardly, you'd tell me, wouldn't you?"

"Maybe. What qualifies as dastardly?"

He snorted a laugh. "To be honest, a hit man wouldn't surprise me."

This was a bit much, even for Jacqueline. "Wouldn't it be easier to get a divorce?"

"She doesn't want that," he said with a frown. "I think having me killed would hold a much greater appeal."

"I doubt it. Have you ever considered just avoiding her?"

"What, pretend she doesn't exist and start another life with someone else?"

"It's been done. I've heard of men maintaining two or three families."

He shook his head. "Too much trouble—aside from being illegal. Besides, I've already got a full-time job; I don't need another one—which is what that would be like. But, really, is having just one family too much to ask?"

"No," Terri replied. "Although lots of people don't have them."

"I can't argue with that." He took the bottle of sunscreen from her and smeared a little more on his chest.

Nice pecs… The abs aren't bad, either…

"I just never thought I'd be one of them."

"One doesn't, I believe."

"Meaning what?" He rose up, glaring at her. "That other people can see why, just not the person involved? So, what, am I too blind to see why Jackie won't have my children? Is there something wrong with me that I don't know about?"

Terri ran a sweeping glance from his head to his toes and didn't find a single thing wrong with him, unless the problem was something that didn't show. Like insanity. She considered this for a moment before dismissing it completely. No, he wasn't crazy. Jacqueline would have had a field day with it if he had been. "I think it's more along the lines of something that you don't see about her."

He chewed on that for several moments before nodding somewhat reluctantly and lying back down. "You might be right."

Why did he keep trying? He could divorce his wife on some grounds or other, and then be free to marry someone else. He'd already wasted an inordinate amount of time on her. Then again, she might have actually made that hit man threat, which would make anyone think twice before rocking the boat. And she *was* beautiful. Maybe he *did* want her genes. After all the "ugly" cracks Jacqueline had made about him, perhaps he thought his bloodline needed improving. How in the world had Ben and Jacqueline gotten together to begin with? She'd never heard that story.

Terri glanced up and saw that her two eye-candy guys were back again. As they walked toward the hotel, Terri could've sworn the shorter one winked at her—which was certainly a first. For one brief, shining moment she forgot all about Ben and Jacqueline and thought that perhaps—just perhaps—something might come of it. But, no. It would never happen. She wasn't the kind to delude herself about what was possible and what wasn't.

"You're starting to get a little pink," Ben observed. "Maybe we should get out of the sun for a while."

Terri doubted that the sun was the only factor involved in her skin tone because she'd felt a bit of a blush when "Shorty" winked at her. Still, it was an excellent excuse to follow them. She might even be able to discover where they went.

"Good idea," she replied, and began gathering up her gear.

"Think it's worth trying to check in yet?"

"Maybe." She shrugged.

"If not, how about some lunch?"

She darted a glance in the direction Shorty and Slim had taken just in time to see them dive into the pool. *So, they're staying at the same hotel.* The irony of her predicament almost made her laugh out loud. Terri was supposed to be there to keep Ben from getting too intimate with Jacqueline, and Shorty and Slim would help divert her attention from Ben. She wasn't really in love with Ben, anyway. How could she be? She barely knew him. Her response to him was animal attraction, nothing more. Jacqueline was just selfish enough not to want anyone else to have Ben, whether she wanted him for herself or not. She would keep him, and Terri would get fired. Although she could have gotten another job fairly easily, it *was* a pretty good job.

"Terri," Ben said impatiently. "Lunch? What about lunch?" He turned, following her gaze. "What are you looking at?"

"The pool. I think I'll go for a swim. I need to cool off a bit."

The hot, wet bodies of Shorty and Slim drew her eyes like a magnet.

"Hey, what's wrong with you all of a sudden?" Ben asked anxiously. "I know we got off on the wrong foot, but we were having a good time out there. What are you, manic-depressive or something?"

"No."

"Well, then, what's the matter?"

"Nothing."

"Oh, no, wait, I get it," he said after a moment's reflection. "You didn't like it when I got so close to you. Hey, can I help it if you look totally hot in a bikini? Give me a break. I'm only human."

"You made me buy it."

"But you could have gotten more than one," he reasoned. "I would've paid for it."

"And then you would've picked on me until I wore this one, wouldn't you?"

"Well, maybe," he admitted with an impish grin.

Terri had reached the pool by then, and she halted at the edge, turning to face him. He was a good bit taller, and she had to tip her head back to look him in the eye.

"Look," she said firmly. "You are not my boss, my husband, or my boyfriend. You are my employer's husband, and letting you buy me a bikini is just a little beyond the limits of what is acceptable. It's bad enough that I bought it at your insistence. I will not do anything further to jeopardize my job, so if you've got any more ideas about what I should or shouldn't wear, please keep them to yourself. I'm here to work, and when this week is over, I start my real vacation— that is, if I still have a job. Either way, I'd rather not spend my time arguing with you. Understand?"

Terri didn't give him a chance to reply, but turned on her heel and headed toward the lobby. As she passed the far end of the pool, she caught a glimpse of Shorty bobbing in the water. He'd undoubtedly heard every word and seemed oddly pleased.

Several moments went by before she heard Ben calling out for her to wait, but she ignored him and kept right on going.

Terri was surprised she'd been able to stand up to him like that. He was probably right, though. If men were, indeed, animals, she'd simply never encountered a stag in rut before—or triggered that response. Ben's behavior might have been perfectly acceptable to an experienced woman, but experience with men was something she didn't have. The way she'd put suntan lotion on him could have been construed as provocative, but she knew better now.

She ought to explain her inexperience to Ben and apologize. And she would, if he ever spoke to her again. Hopefully, he would understand. After giving it some thought, she decided that she might have been making a mountain out of a molehill. Some married men probably still liked to flirt. After all, he hadn't said much that was truly out of line and his comment that she looked hot in a bikini should have been enough to make her forgive him for just about anything. At least he hadn't said she had to be naked by two o'clock.

Still, although Terri was momentarily flattered, she had a feeling she was right in the middle of a disaster waiting to happen.

Chapter 5

Terri refused to be a part of that disaster. Jacqueline could be ruthless when it suited her, and she wasn't about to give her an excuse to aim her sights in Terri's direction. She'd kept her boss happy for a good long while, and dear, sweet Benjamin wasn't going to make her change that. There were plenty of other men around to divert her attention from Ben, many of them younger and more available. If what happened in Myrtle Beach stayed in Myrtle Beach, so much the better. She wasn't necessarily looking for a lifelong commitment anyway. She only had to be there with Ben whenever Jacqueline was around. The rest of the time, she could ignore him— and maybe even have a little fun.

Terri didn't need Ben or his car. As a tough New Yorker, the thought of walking wherever she wanted to go didn't bother her a bit. Besides, if she played her cards right, Shorty and Slim might give her a ride.

She stalked into the lobby and was about to check on the room, when she remembered that her purse was locked in the rental car, and also that Ben had the damned keys.

So much for my good intentions.

Spinning around, she crashed right into Ben, smudging her glasses on his recently oiled chest. "Sorry! I didn't mean to—"

"What? Put me in my place or run into me?"

His tone of voice gave nothing away. Neither did his face—and not only because he was a total blur from the goop that was now smeared all over her lenses.

Taking a deep breath, she tried to steady her voice. "I'm sorry for running into you. And I'm sorry I felt the *need* to put you in your place. I'm also very sorry if I've given you the wrong idea." She stared down at the highly polished floor—anywhere but at his face.

How can I possibly make him understand?

"It's just that I've never..." What should she say at this juncture? That she'd never been touched? Never been kissed? Was still a virgin at the age of twenty-eight? Didn't even have a clue as to what sex might be like?

"Hung out on the beach with such an irresistible hunk before?"

His tone was unmistakable. He knew she'd been angry and was attempting to tease her into a better mood.

A good sign.

Taking off her glasses, she looked up at him. He appeared to be smiling, although as bad as her vision was, he could have been wearing a grin or a snarl. She preferred to believe it was a smile. After giving a brief thought to what Constance might have said in reply, Terri decided that anything she would have said would have only gotten him started all over again.

"A hunk? Where? I didn't see one." Gathering up the corner of her towel, she began to wipe off the smudges. "Just let me get these glasses cleaned and I'll—"

"Oh, very funny!" he snapped. "Come on, let's see if the room is ready."

It was. Pleased that they'd made it past that obstacle, Terri waited while Ben went to get the car, which was parked some distance from the hotel. As chilly as it was in the lobby, it wasn't long before she was shivering in her wet suit—what little there was of it.

She asked the desk clerk to tell Ben she'd gone out to the hot tub, which was near the pool. Easing herself down into the hot, frothy water, she leaned back against the side, laid her glasses on the edge, and closed her eyes. Bone tired, she decided that this was what she should have done to begin with since it was so much more relaxing than the beach.

Ben. What on earth was she going to do with him for a week?

He made her crazy. In spite of everything, she liked him. She was supposed to keep him occupied, couldn't have him—wouldn't have known what to do with him anyway—but he seemed like he…

Oh hell. What a mess!

A shadow passed over her shuttered eyes, accompanied by soft male voices, their conversation mixed with laughter. Terri opened one eye—just a slit. Shorty and Slim had joined her in the tub.

Even without her glasses, Terri had no difficulty recognizing them at that range, and they were still cute, if a bit fuzzy. Should she speak to them? Or smile? She'd never paid much attention to men before. *My mistake.* These two were perfectly adorable, and she watched them covertly as they laughed and moved around in front of the jets, sending the spray shooting high above their heads.

Two small children joined them, and she moved over to make room, bringing her closer to the two men. Shorty said something, and being totally out of focus, it took Terri a moment to realize that he was addressing *her.*

"Is this place open at night?" he asked, indicating the pool area.

"I don't know. I just got here."

"So did we," he said. "Are you staying long?"

"A week." *A long, torturous week with the boss from hell and her equally devilish husband.* If Terri died at the end of the week, she would surely pass straight into heaven, having already been through purgatory.

"So are we," Slim said. "I guess we'll be seeing you around then."

She nodded. "Probably so."

"Terri, are you ready to check in?" Ben's voice sounded from directly above her.

"Sure." She nodded at Shorty and Slim and donned her glasses. They were even cuter in focus. "Nice meeting you guys."

"See you later," Shorty said. His smile would have dazzled anyone. Perfect teeth, dimples, and *everything.*

They checked in, explaining to the desk clerk that Jacqueline would be arriving later, and then an energetic bellman helped them transport their luggage up to the room. By this time, Terri was hungry enough to wish she'd taken Ben up on his lunch offer.

Having researched the hotel for Jacqueline, she knew what amenities there were, but she was still unprepared for the reality of it. A two-bedroom condo on the sixth floor, it had a full kitchen, two full bathrooms, a living room with floor to ceiling windows that faced south and east, three televisions, free Internet, and an oceanfront balcony with a view to die for. It even had a washer and dryer. Easily twice the size of her own apartment, Terri had never been in such a beautiful, spacious hotel room in her life.

The view might have been fabulous, but the bed was calling her. She'd slept very little the night before and had been at the airport by four-thirty. With all the sun and surf and turmoil on top of that, she was beginning to fade.

"So, what do you have to do to get ready for Jackie?" Ben asked. "Turn down the sheets and plump up her pillows?"

Terri ignored his snide inflection. "Yes. Are you hungry?"

"Hey, now, I just asked if you wanted lunch, and you ignored me."

"True. But I *am* hungry."

"Well, if you'll tell me what you want on your pizza, I'll order one." He waved a flier at her and snickered. "It says here that this place has the best pizza on the beach."

Terri couldn't blame Ben for his sarcasm. As a fellow New Yorker, she shared the belief the food everywhere else in the world was substandard, especially pizza. "Pepperoni, black olives, mushrooms, extra cheese and jalapeños."

His eyebrows flicked up. "Well, I guess we can leave the peppers off half of it."

"Okay."

"Or I can pick them off and give them to you."

"Fine."

"What do you want to drink?"

"Something cold."

His eyebrows flicked again, which seemed to be his preferred method for registering surprise. "Well, you're easy."

Terri shook her head. "Not really."

He gazed at her, clearly puzzled. "Do you realize that you hardly ever say more than two words at a time if you can help it—unless you're telling someone off, that is. Do I have to keep you pissed all the time to have a decent conversation with you?"

"Guess so."

His eyebrows went up again. He was going to develop a permanent twitch if he hung around her much longer. By the end of the week, they would probably be stuck in the "up" position.

"When does Jackie's flight arrive?"

"Six."

"Damn! Now we're down to *one* word!"

"Sorry," she said with an apologetic shrug.

"Well, don't be," he said. "It's probably my fault, anyway."

"Not really."

"Well then what is it?"

She shrugged without saying anything, and Ben made a sudden movement as if he was about to give his hair a yank. Obviously he didn't like quiet women, but she did like his curly hair. She didn't want to be the one to make him pull it out by the roots.

Shorty's hair was curly too, and he was cuter than Slim. If they spent most of their vacation hanging around the hotel, she might see more of them. Maybe they wouldn't mind if she wasn't talkative.

Ben was frowning again. "What are you thinking about?"

"Nothing much."

"Are you saying that your mind is a blank?"

"No."

"Would you do me a favor?"

"Sure." *Anything but hanky-panky.*

"Go take a shower and rest for a while and I'll let you know when the pizza gets here."

"Okay."

Since that was exactly what Terri had in mind, she didn't argue. Besides, it gave him the opportunity to tell her what to do. People had always seemed to enjoy bossing her around, possibly because they found her silence unnerving and it got her out of the way. Her own mother had done the same. Ben was no different.

The water in the shower was hot and invigorating. Lathering her skin with the creamy soap, she drifted off into a blissful state of self-indulgence, knowing that she not only wouldn't have to pay the utility bill, but she probably wouldn't run out of hot water, no matter how long she stayed in there.

Drying herself with the thick, snowy towels was another decadent luxury. They were even folded into little fans, and there was a whole stack of them too. No wonder Jacqueline had always insisted on four or five-star hotels. There was, indeed, a difference. Terri wrapped her hair up in one of those amazing towels, snuggled into her robe and keeled over onto the nearest bed.

ജ

Ben had never met a woman quite like Terri. If there was anyone who was the direct opposite of his wife, she was it.

Must be why I like her.

Ben had tried. He truly had, but there was simply no denying the fact that his wife was not the woman he thought he'd married. In a world of hasty marriage and easy divorce, he'd thought their marriage would be different. And it was different—as in not a true marriage at all. It was more along the lines of a marriage of convenience. Jackie's convenience, not his.

He knew he'd behaved badly toward Terri—hell, he'd practically had his dick wedged between her buns—but when he'd seen her in that bikini, well…something inside him sort of…snapped. He'd been reminded that there were other women in the world aside from his wife. Women who were soft and warm and, yes, made his dick hard. He hadn't been affected by a woman in ages, though, once upon a time, Jackie had done it quite easily. When they'd first met, she'd been the hottest, sexiest woman he could imagine, and he'd followed her around like a lovesick puppy until she finally took pity on him and agreed to a date.

A date was all it had been. No sex at all until after they were married. He thought she might loosen up eventually, but she never did. Ben had blamed himself for years, but in the back of his mind, he knew it wasn't true. Jackie refused to acknowledge the problem, handling the situation by distancing herself further and further. What he couldn't understand was why she kept stringing him along. A person with an ounce of kindness would have divorced him long ago. Instead, Jackie had kept him dangling in limbo when he would have welcomed something more definite, even if it was a not-so-fond farewell and a handshake.

Picking up the phone, he ordered the pizza and then plopped down on the couch. This week would either be the beginning or the end of his relationship with Jackie. He didn't believe in cheating, although it would have been an easy thing to do. Jackie would never have known and probably wouldn't have cared.

Early on, they'd both been busy building their careers and working too hard to even think about having children. In fact, they'd agreed not to, but lately, he'd keyed on the fact that something was seriously missing from his life.

Now that his reputation as an architect was established, he could back off and focus on the projects he truly wanted to do rather than taking on every job he was offered. He was thirty-eight years old. If life truly began at forty, he didn't have much of a life to look forward to—unless something changed…drastically.

The time he and Terri had spent together made him realize exactly what he was missing. He wanted a family. He wanted to play on the beach with his own children. And he wanted a wife he could have fun with and who actually *liked* sex. It shouldn't have been too much to wish for.

The doorbell rang and he went and paid for the pizza. The delivery boy was fresh-faced and young. He'd been like that himself once upon a time.

What the hell happened to me?

ஐௐ

Terri awoke to the heavenly smell of hot pizza. Her stomach growled as the aroma wafted over her in waves, as though someone was flapping the lid on the box.

"The pizza's here," that someone whispered. "Are you hungry?"

"Um-hm."

"Guess you don't talk in your sleep, either," Ben commented. "Get up, now. You've got to have everything perfect for Jackie. She'll be here any minute."

Terri didn't move, nor did she open her eyes. "No she won't. It doesn't take that long to get a pizza delivered."

"Ah, ha! You said a whole sentence! *Two* of them!"

Terri sat up and squinted at him peevishly. "I thought men didn't like chatterboxes."

"Generally speaking, most people fall somewhere between the silent type and the chatterbox." He sat down on the side of the bed. "I've known plenty of people who will talk your ear off, but I've never met anyone quite like you."

Part of the reason Terri didn't know what to say to him was because she'd never met anyone quite like him, either. The other part was that she was there under false pretenses and had taken an arrow through the heart because of him.

It's a wonder I can talk to him at all.

"Here, have a drink." He offered her a can of soda. "We'll eat it right here. You seem to be more talkative in the bedroom."

Terri chose to ignore the implication. "Not really. I can talk just as well in the living room as I can in here."

"I think you're wrong about that." He selected a slice of pizza and handed it over. "No need to tell *you* not to talk with your mouth full, is there?"

She shook her head and took a bite. It was delicious. *I guess they really can make good pizza outside of New York.*

"Now, don't bite my head off for saying this," he began. "But you're really cute when you're asleep."

Meaning that she wasn't cute when she was awake? Terri chewed on that for a moment before swallowing and saying, "So are you."

"When—? Oh, you mean on the beach. I think I might have dozed off for a minute or two."

"Yeah."

He let out a groan. "Oh, here we go again. *Please* talk to me. I don't want to spend the whole week talking to myself."

"Do we *have* to talk?"

"Well, Jackie said you'd keep me company during the day. I assumed that we might actually, you know…*talk.*"

"I'll try," she said, although without much conviction. "This is just me."

He was silent for a moment. "Okay," he said finally. "I can accept that. But you have to realize that it's a little odd."

Terri thought he was about to say annoying or irritating or rude or any of the other remarks which had been made in regard to her peculiar speech patterns over the years. *Odd* was actually one of the milder descriptions. Funny, but Ben was someone who made her wish she really *could* be chatty and witty and entertaining. It shouldn't have mattered, but somehow it did. It would be difficult having to keep up the other end of a week-long conversation, particularly when she couldn't tell him what she was thinking. It almost made her look forward to Jacqueline's arrival. With her around, Terri wouldn't have to say much at all. They could talk to each other.

Of course, Jacqueline didn't *want* to talk to Ben, which why

Terri was there to begin with. In desperation, she kept stuffing pizza into her mouth and chewing it and chewing it and chewing it until there was nothing left. He wouldn't expect her to talk with her mouth full, but the point finally came when she couldn't hold another bite. Then she realized that instead of losing weight on this vacation, she would probably gain some. *Great!* She wanted to cry, but then she would have had to explain her tears to Ben. She could plead jet-lag, but she hadn't crossed a time zone. Was there such a thing as latitude-lag? This might have made a stimulating topic for conversation if it wasn't so idiotic.

After she finished eating, she went into her bathroom and closed the door. Surely, he wouldn't expect her to talk from there.

But he did.

"Dry your hair, and then we'll go to the grocery," he called out. "We need to get some snacks and stuff for breakfast. That way we won't have to go out all the time."

"Okay," she said, raising her voice to be sure he heard. Then she switched on the blow dryer. This was getting better and better. If they never went out, she'd be spending even more time with him, either on the beach, or in the room. Hanging out with Shorty and Slim was looking more appealing all the time.

Chapter 6

Going to the grocery with Ben was like speech therapy. His questions were endless. What did she want, what did she like, could she cook, did she *mind* cooking, and if so, then would it matter if he fixed his own breakfast? What kind of dishwashing liquid did she use? Was she allergic to anything? Did she like beer, or did she prefer wine? Coffee or tea? Two percent or skim? Cheddar or American? White or wheat? Mustard or mayo? What made it even more hilarious was, that Terri could answer all his questions with a nod or just a couple of words—he wasn't making her talk more at all. She wondered if he was altering his own style of communication to suit hers, or if this was typical for him—but, of course, she didn't ask.

After they'd finished loading up the car, she tuned the car radio to a classic rock station and turned up the volume. He talked anyway.

Her break finally came when he dropped her off at the hotel with their purchases and then went to park the car. It was a bit of a struggle to carry everything, but she made it to the elevator just as Shorty and Slim were getting off.

Shorty actually seemed pleased to see her. "Hey, it's you again! Would you like some help?"

Yep. Still cute up close and in focus. "Um, sure."

They each took a handful, leaving Terri with nothing to carry but her purse, and got back on the elevator.

"What floor?" Slim asked, his finger hovering over the control panel.

"Six," she replied.

"We'll ride up with you and carry this to your room, if you like," Shorty said.

In the glare of his blinding smile, Terri nodded even more dumbly than usual.

"You *do* remember us, don't you? We saw you on the beach and again in the hot tub."

She nodded again, although just how they thought she would have forgotten them was beyond her comprehension. They were nothing if not memorable.

"Where are you from?" he asked.

"New York."

"Wow, that's a long way!" he exclaimed. "How long did it take you?"

"Two hours."

Shorty stared at her in disbelief.

"She flew," Slim said, rolling his eyes. Gesturing at Shorty with a thumb, he added, "He's not the sharpest tool in the shed."

"Cute, though." Terri couldn't believe she'd said it aloud, but she must have, because he thanked her. Emboldened by this amazing turn of events, she asked, "Where are you guys from?"

"North Carolina," Slim replied. "We come here every summer."

"This is my first time. I'm here with my boss and her husband."

Shorty's eyes lit up. "So, the guy you were with on the beach isn't your husband, then?"

Terri was pretty sure they'd heard the exchange between her and Ben by the pool, but thought perhaps they didn't want to admit to eavesdropping. "No."

The two of them traded a look that should have made her extremely wary, but didn't for some reason. Maybe it was because she wasn't in New York.

The elevator stopped on the sixth floor, and she reached out to take the bags from them.

"We'll carry them to your room if you want," Slim offered.

Now, she was suspicious. They were being too nice. They

wanted something. "That's all right. I can manage."

"Okay," Shorty said agreeably, transferring the bags back to Terri. "See you on the beach!"

The elevator doors closed, and she shook her head, mentally chastising herself for being so distrusting of a pair of very nice, helpful, friendly people. They were just a couple of guys on vacation, and staying in a rather expensive hotel, which probably meant they had money. Nice boys from North Carolina, not criminals. Of course, they might only be pretending to stay at that hotel while they were looking for their next victim. Or they might have paid for their rooms with money they'd stolen from unsuspecting women who, dazzled by their charms, had let their guard down. Terri checked her purse and bags when she got to the room. Everything was in order. All of Ben's talk about hit men must've had her on edge.

She was putting the groceries away when she heard the door open.

"Hello!" Jacqueline called out. "Anybody home?"

"Yes." Terri walked over to the hallway and waved. "Need any help?"

"Oh, no," she replied. "This nice young man is helping me."

Terri froze for a moment thinking that Shorty and Slim had found another victim, but it was only the hotel bellman. Terri went to help anyway, since she knew that Jacqueline hadn't meant a word of what she'd just said. If she didn't lend a hand, it would come back to haunt her someday. Subtly, of course, but it *would* happen, just like death and taxes and all that other crap.

The bellman deposited the bags in the room Terri indicated. Jacqueline gave him a tip, and he left.

"Is Ben here?" she whispered as soon as the door closed behind him.

"No, we just got back from the grocery. He's parking the car."

"Any problems?"

"No." Unless she were to count getting shot at by a chubby

cherub, having Ben make her cry, insist that she buy a bikini, have several arguments with her, and try to talk her to death. And say things like she had good hands, was hot in that bikini, looked cute when she was asleep, and had odd speech patterns. Terri knew better than to mention those. They were her problems, not Jacqueline's, whether they involved Ben or not.

Jacqueline nodded and glanced around the room. With an untoward degree of horror, she gasped, "I'm *sharing* a room? With *him?"*

Terri hadn't expected this part—well, maybe she *had,* but still, they *were* married. "You'd rather not?"

"The idea was to keep him away from me!" she said indignantly. "I can't be in the same bedroom with him!"

Which made Terri wonder if she ever had been. Who *were* these people? Were they aliens? She hoped Jacqueline had a reason all worked out in advance that would placate Ben, because she certainly didn't. The pod-person idea came back to her. Terri didn't want to sleep in the same room with a pod-person. Perhaps Ben wouldn't either. Then again, it was possible that neither of them had seen *Invasion of the Body Snatchers* and wouldn't understand the dangers involved.

"No problem. I'll take care of it." Terri would have to move her stuff into the living room and sleep on the sofa bed, and then move Ben's things into what had been her room because it was a given that Jacqueline would want the larger bathroom. Which undoubtedly meant that Terri would end up being the one to share a bathroom with Ben.

This was so unreal! These people were *married,* for heaven's sake! If that was what marriage was like, she wanted no part of it.

She went back to the kitchen and put the rest of the groceries away while Jacqueline busied herself with the arduous task of checking out the view from the balcony. Terri was in the process of gathering up Ben's belongings to carry into the other room when he returned.

"You wouldn't *believe* where I had to go to park the damned car! There's a parking garage two blocks over, and I wound up on the top floor. It's worse than New York!" He paused for a moment as he took in the nature of Terri's task. "What are you doing?"

"Moving you," she replied. "Jacqueline is here."

"And she wants the smaller bedroom? That's odd, I would have thought—"

"No, she wants this one," Terri stated flatly. "To *herself.*"

Ben recoiled as though he'd been slapped. At that moment, for two cents Terri would've hired a hit man to go after Jacqueline. This was no way to treat your husband—whether you liked him or not—especially in front of someone who was a virtual stranger to him. Keeping him occupied was one thing; this was something altogether different. It was not only cruel, but humiliating as well.

"Did she say *why* she doesn't want to share a room with me?"

Terri toyed with the idea of telling him the truth about why she was there to begin with, but decided against it, shaking her head.

His lips thinned, and he exhaled like a bull about to charge. "What about you?" he asked with a sardonic laugh. "Are *we* sharing a room?"

"There's a sofa bed in the living room."

"I'll sleep there, then. You shouldn't have to." He took another deep breath and blew it out slowly. "Obviously this whole thing was a bad idea."

You don't know the half of it. "I'll take the sofa bed," Terri insisted. "Sometimes I stay up late working, and the Internet connection is out there. They don't have wireless."

If his incredulous expression was anything to go by, Terri didn't think he believed her, but he nodded anyway.

"Is it…would it be okay if I share your bathroom?" she asked. "It's got a door into the hallway. If you close the other door from your side I shouldn't disturb you."

"It would serve Jackie right if I refused," he snapped. "This is ridiculous! Where the hell is she, anyway?"

"On the balcony."

As he stormed off, Terri told herself it was none of her business, and carried his suitcase into what had been her room. *So much for the posh hotel.* Terri had known things would change when Jacqueline arrived, she just hadn't realized how much. At least they hadn't unpacked yet, which was some consolation. It was no big deal, really.

Of course, moving luggage around wasn't the only issue. A husband and wife *should* share a room, so it would serve Jacqueline right if Terri *did* sleep with him. Then she realized that she could do just that and Jacqueline would probably never know or even give a damn. The master bedroom was at the end of the hallway by the entrance. Terri could sneak back to Ben's room from her undoubtedly lumpy sofa bed and climb right in with him—quite easily, in fact. Or she could sleep in the other bed, since there were two in each room. *I should just do—*

Her mind stopped right there as a rather chilling thought struck her.

This is the plan!

Jacqueline would make Ben so miserable that he'd start looking to Terri for comfort, and then she would catch him screwing around and have grounds for divorce—on *her* terms. She probably even had a camera. She would take him to the cleaners, and Terri would be the one left holding the ticket. It was devious. It was clever. And given what had already happened between her and Ben, it might even work. Jacqueline must've been waiting for this opportunity to present itself for years. Then Terri remembered that Jacqueline wasn't that smart and would never be able to concoct such a scheme on her own.

Perhaps Ben had. Jacqueline had said he'd been badgering her to have a baby. Maybe he thought she was refusing him because she had a lover and was here for a rendezvous. Suspecting that she'd been cuckolding him, he'd insisted on coming along just so he could catch her and her boyfriend, and then take *her* to the cleaners.

Terri didn't believe that, either. The only plan that made any sense at all was that they'd both gotten together to drive Terri insane. Of course, there was no motive for *that*, because neither of them had anything to gain by turning her into a lunatic. At least Terri didn't think they had. Then again, she could have been wrong…

Terri shook her head and chuckled grimly. Here she was, moving stuff from room to room and making up detective stories while those two idiots were out there on the balcony, probably having a big fight when they could be in each other's arms. What a stupid, senseless waste of time! They should be in that bedroom down the hall making whoopee and babies and God knows what else. As it was, Terri would consider her mission accomplished if they didn't push each other off the balcony. And if they did, with Terri's luck, she'd probably end up being accused of a double homicide. Of course, she had no motive—except that she might have pushed Jacqueline off right after she'd done the same thing to Ben. Terri could see the headline…

Executive Kills Husband, Assistant Kills Executive

Terri figured she could always use the insanity plea, which would have been quite believable under the circumstances. No one would blame Terri if she got the right witnesses to testify on her behalf. There were probably dozens of people who wished Jacqueline dead, because if her boss had any conscience at all, Terri had never seen any evidence of it. Jacqueline had a different slant on things and had a self-serving reason for just about everything she did. It was a mystery to Terri how she justified her actions on a daily basis—or how she slept at night.

Having finished the job, Terri wandered back out to the kitchen, only then remembering that she was supposed to keep Ben away from Jacqueline. And what had she done? She'd sent him out to the balcony to look for her—and with murder in his eyes, no less! She was probably well on her way to getting fired.

As she entered the kitchen/living room area, Terri could see that they were still out there. Arguing. She could hear their raised voices through the glass door, but couldn't understand what they were saying. Taking a deep breath for courage, she slapped a smile on her lips and slid the door open.

"Isn't this a fabulous view?" she asked. "It made me a little dizzy the first time I came out here, but I'll bet you can see twenty miles in any direction!"

Terri's intrusion caught Ben in mid-tirade, and he stared at her with disbelief so complete she almost laughed out loud. Jacqueline eyed her with a certain amount of relief mingled with annoyance. *Oh, yes, I can expect a tongue-lashing from each of them.* Too bad she couldn't get them both at the same time and get it over with. Hanging out with Shorty and Slim was her best option. Maybe they had an extra room—or an extra bed. Even *sharing* a bed with them wouldn't be a bad thing. A bit crowded, perhaps, but certainly more friendly. It might even turn out to be fun…

With that cheery thought in mind, she went on, "Jacqueline, your room is ready for you if you'd like to lie down for a while. There are snacks and drinks, too. I see from your itinerary that the conference is hosting a couple of dinners, but I've checked out the restaurants, and I doubt if there's a bad one in town. Some of them take reservations, but most don't. Do you have any preference for this evening?"

Ben gaped at Terri as though she'd sprouted wings. Jacqueline obviously recognized her standard executive assistant mode and nodded. "Seafood. Pick one. I'm sure it will be lovely."

"The buffet seems to be the most popular type," Terri went on. "But there are others that offer more of a fine dining experience."

"Let's do the buffet," Ben said. "I don't feel like getting all dressed up."

From the way Jacqueline jumped, Ben might've just materialized from another dimension. For a brief moment, Terri thought Jacqueline would disagree with him, but she didn't.

"There's even one called Benjamin's," Terri said with the barest hint of a sidelong glance at Ben. "It's supposed to be pretty good."

Jacqueline didn't refuse simply on the basis of the name, which Terri thought she might do, but merely nodded and went to lie down, asking to be called in an hour.

Ben waited until the door to the bedroom closed before rounding on Terri. "How can you act like that when she just bumped you out of your bed?"

"She didn't bump *me*," Terri reminded him. "She bumped *you*. And keep your voice down, please. I don't want her to think we're talking about her."

"Why the hell *shouldn't* we be talking about her?" He still sounded angry, but he *did* lower his voice. "She may be my wife, but I'm under no illusions that she gives a shit about anyone but herself. She ought to expect people to talk about her—to her face or behind her back."

"She may be your *wife,* but she's my *boss.* So, if it's all the same to you, I believe I'd rather not get fired while I'm on vacation."

He rolled his eyes and shot her a grim smile. "Sorry, I keep forgetting that. I feel like I'm talking to her sister instead of her assistant."

Was that a compliment or a slap in the face? "Look, just do me a favor and don't talk about her while she's here. The rest of the time doesn't matter. You can tell me anything you like and I'll listen. I'm a good listener, remember?"

"Yeah, I know. Hey, how come you can talk to her in more than one or two words, but you can't with me?"

She had, actually, but apparently he hadn't been paying attention. "It's different."

"How?"

"I don't know you."

"What do you mean? We've spent almost a whole day together, which is more than I can say for the time I've spent with you-know-who lately. Hey, why don't you share the room with me? Jacqueline obviously won't care, and I feel terrible making you sleep on a sofa bed. There's a perfectly good bed in there for you. I…oh, shit, I don't know," he mumbled. "I'll shut up now. You're probably sick to death of hearing me talk, anyway."

Terri had a feeling she wasn't going to get much sleep on this trip, no matter where she spent the night and no matter how much he talked. "You should ask Jacqueline about that."

He snorted with disgust. "I don't have to. She already told me I should share the room with you. She had the audacity to say it was because she didn't want to disturb me when she left so early in the mornings. I was screaming at her, and she just smiled that honey-sweet smile and said she was only thinking of *me*. Hell, if she was only thinking of me, she might actually let me f—" He broke off there. "You don't really want to hear this crap, do you?"

Terri shrugged. "I hear all kinds of stuff, and you can even say the whole f-word if you like. I've heard some things that would astonish you. People seem to feel the need to fill in the silences whenever they're around me, and they usually end up spilling their guts."

"You want me to spill my guts? Well, here goes: I've only had physical contact with my wife once in the last two years. Do you have any idea how that makes a man feel?"

Terri could have topped his story without even trying, but she was in listening mode. "No."

"Well, it's not good! I hate to admit this, but I knew Jackie didn't want children when we got married. I can't say she lied about it, and I wasn't sure I wanted kids, either. But I thought she might change her mind someday, like I did. Honest to God, people who get married to get their green card have more love and affection between them than we do! It was okay at first, but after a while it just withered away and died. She doesn't want a divorce because she says it'll ruin her career. I don't believe that for a second, but I can't see any other reason why she feels that way."

"I can. Being married keeps the other men in line—up to a point. You wouldn't believe what goes on around the office—well, maybe you would. And she's so beautiful…"

"Yeah, I know," he said wearily. "*Believe* me, I know."

Chapter 7

Dinner was a rather odd affair. In excellent form after her nap, Jacqueline was downright captivating. Terri could easily see how she'd managed to keep Ben hanging on for so long, grateful for whatever little scraps of attention she was willing to give him. At one point, she even gave him a hug.

Terri wanted to slap her. Jacqueline obviously didn't truly care for him, and it was cruel of her to lead him on. However, when they got back to the hotel, she didn't relent on the sleeping arrangements, saying nothing other than that she had to be up early the next day and was going straight to bed.

Alone with Ben, Terri sat at the dining table, ostensibly working, when in reality she was surfing the Net while he watched television. After a while, he shut it off and sat there on the couch, staring off into space. When he finally closed his eyes, she stopped pretending to work and gazed at him. They'd been together for almost an entire day, and twenty-four hours ago she hadn't even met him. She'd seen most of his moods now, had seen him smile, heard him laugh, witnessed his anger, and heard him swear…

A slight twinge marked the spot where Cupid's arrow had struck her. What if she'd met Ben before Jacqueline entered the picture? Would her life—and his—be any different? Would they be together? And if so, would they have children? Would they be in Myrtle Beach for a family vacation?

Terri let her mind roam, imagining Ben playing in the surf with the little ones who would squeal as they ran from the waves and then shriek with laughter when he snatched them up in his arms. He would return to where she sat on her beach towel in the sand, kissing her perhaps, or simply giving her a smile.

Such thoughts were a rare occurrence for Terri, and she had Ben to thank for them. She could never say thank you to his face, though. It would have sounded silly.

What would she say to him if she could? *Leave Jacqueline and be mine. I'll give you anything you want if you'll only share your love with me and forget her.* Making a man happy wasn't something Terri had ever attempted—or had any idea how to go about doing— but somehow, with *him,* she was willing to give it her best shot.

Resting her elbow on the table, she leaned forward with chin in hand as she drank in every detail. The steady rise and fall of his chest, his odd little sniffle now and then, the slope of his brow where it met his temple, the sensuous curve of his lips, the firm line of his chin. Oh, yes, she could love this man as much as he needed to be loved—even though she'd had no experience whatsoever. After consistently meeting Jacqueline's high standards, pleasing him would be a piece of cake. Unfortunately, fate had sent them all down a different path.

Her heart filled with longing—an emotion she'd seldom felt before. Quite honestly, she'd wanted very little in her life. She had what she needed, of course, but never coveted anything, never had a desire that couldn't be fulfilled, or a craving that couldn't be satisfied. Until now.

Terri didn't delude herself into thinking that Ben would ever look at her with the same degree of desire. He was married to a very beautiful, successful woman, and though he had no illusions about Jacqueline's character, he *had* stayed married to her, and he still wanted to have a family. True, it might have been his only option since Jacqueline didn't want to end the marriage, but why did she insist on perpetuating the myth that they were a happy couple?

It might have been something to do with the division of property in a divorce, or that she feared Ben might come out the winner—although Terri didn't see why he would. Jacqueline's refusal to admit failure probably played a part, but couldn't explain everything. The one thing Terri *did* know was that neither of them seemed happy, and at the moment, neither was she.

She glanced at her watch. *Eleven thirty*. Ben was obviously tired and should go to bed, if for no other reason than to allow her to get in hers, since he happened to be sitting on it. Of course, he may have only been making sure *she* didn't sleep there. Hoping he was a light sleeper, she made more noise than necessary as she got ready for bed, but he slept like a stone.

"Ben?"

Although his eyelids twitched, there was no other response. She gave him a little poke on the shoulder and called his name again. A quirky little smile flitted across his lips, disappearing completely as he opened his eyes. What had he been dreaming about? Then she felt a pang as she realized that he must have thought she was his wife, coming to invite him to her bed. All she could think about was what a slap in the face the sight of her in a frumpy cotton gown would be to a man expecting the vision of loveliness that was Jacqueline.

She choked back tears she had no business shedding. "I want to go to bed."

"Then go," he said. "I'm not moving."

"But—"

"Go," he said again. *"Now."*

Bitter tears were already falling as she left the room—tears that later soaked her pillow. She fell asleep imagining that she was firing arrows into Cupid's cruel heart, forcing him to fall in love with Jacqueline. What a perfect pair they would make.

≈≈≈

Terri awoke the next morning to find Ben asleep in the bed across from her and Jacqueline already up and gone without asking for breakfast or coffee or anything. Neither was there a note on the refrigerator informing Terri that she was fired for sharing a room with Ben—though this might simply have been due to the lack of tape or refrigerator magnets. If asked, Terri would explain the circumstances, but she certainly wasn't going to volunteer any information.

Figuring Ben would want to sleep in, Terri went out on the balcony with a cup of tea. Leaning back in a chair with her feet propped up on the railing, she gazed out at the vast expanse of nothingness. The Atlantic looked different with a southern exposure, although it might simply have been the long stretch of wide, sandy beach. Whatever the reason, the vision gave her a sense of endless possibilities, something she'd never experienced while looking at the sea. It was an odd feeling, as though the space increased the potential for…something...

The soft ocean breeze ruffled her hair as the rising sun cast a dazzling glare on the surface of the sea. *Another day with Ben.* How would she feel when she saw him again? Would her impressions of him from the day before have vanished overnight, or would she feel exactly the same? Would she get hit with another arrow to her heart, or would things simply pick up where they'd left off? She had no idea what to expect.

If only she'd fallen in love a hundred times before and knew exactly what to do, but she had no clue what might happen next. There was no one to discuss it with, either. Constance would have laughed out loud if Terri were to share her feelings.

"You're being silly," Constance would say. "He's just a guy. They're all the same. They have penises, so you can fuck them, just don't ever trust them." Although Constance loved men, she had few illusions about their reliability. Terri disagreed. There had to be a few who were trustworthy. If Ben was one of them, she need have no fears about being alone with him. He would never take liberties with her, whether his wife wanted him or not.

Liberties. Terri chuckled inwardly at the old-fashioned expression. She was out of date, out of sync, and out of her mind…

As she stared out to sea again, her thoughts drifted with the waves. What would she have done if she and Ben had truly been here alone, and there was no Jacqueline? Would she have given him his breakfast in bed, or would she even be up yet, having lingered in the warmth of his embrace to begin the day by making love with him?

The answer to that was quite simple. If there had been no Jacqueline, there would be no Ben. The one eliminated the possibility of the other—no matter how she looked at it.

Where were these peculiar thoughts coming from? Was it poison from Cupid's tainted arrow? Trying to shut them out of her mind, Terri stared at the ocean while the tea grew cold in her cup, wishing only that she'd never met Charles Benjamin Tremaine. That he'd remained a stranger; a face in a photograph on Jacqueline's desk—someone she didn't really know, someone who couldn't affect her this way.

She went back inside and settled herself on the sofa where he'd been sitting the night before, wondering when he had gone to bed and when he would want to get up. Eventually she decided to forget him and go on as if she'd been there alone, eating breakfast in solitude and then wandering out to the beach. With any luck, she might not see him until Jacqueline returned that evening.

A bit later she discovered something else about Ben, which was that the smell of frying bacon would get him out of bed without any trouble at all.

ℂℂ

Ben didn't have to see Terri's empty bed to know she was up. The delicious aromas drifting in from the kitchen were proof enough. After a quick stop in the bathroom, he wandered out to the kitchen, stopping at the threshold.

Dressed in a plain, blue robe with her hair twisted up into a fantail on top of her head, Terri was busily fixing breakfast—for two. While the coffee brewed and the bacon fried, she whipped up the eggs, adding a dollop of soft butter to a second frying pan before pouring in the eggs.

She hadn't left out a single thing. Even the jar of strawberry jam he'd tossed into the grocery basket sat on the counter along with the cream. Jacqueline could never even remember that Ben liked scrambled eggs with cheese, but Terri had obviously noted his preference from the morning before.

She kept right on working while he stood there watching, wishing more than anything that he could take her in his arms and kiss her. Memories of the fun they'd had on the beach returned. He tried not to think about the arguments or the dinner with Jacqueline—who had once again charmed him like the fool he was. When was he ever going to learn?

Terri toasted the bread and then buttered each slice before spreading them with jam. She took up the bacon and eggs, dividing everything into two portions and then poured out a cup of coffee, adding a bit of cream. She did all this without ever looking at him or saying a word.

Picking up his plate and the cup of coffee, she turned and handed it to him.

"Thank you," he said quietly.

Her eyes swept over him as she nodded, her expression as enigmatic as ever. Ben hadn't bothered to change out of the rumpled T-shirt and boxers he'd slept in, nor had he combed his hair. What was she thinking? He'd been rude to her the night before, keeping his eyes glued to the damned television, pretending to ignore her when, in truth, he'd been aware of her every movement, every sigh, even each sip she took of her tea.

Knowing she didn't like to talk, he hadn't pressed her to make conversation, but it was difficult and was even harder now. He was dying to know what went on in her head. When she sat down at the table, he tried to recall what she'd had for breakfast the day before. As far as Ben was concerned, she'd prepared the perfect meal, but was it what she preferred or what *he* liked? At least she was eating it this time.

"I see Jackie left early."

She replied with a nod.

So, I'm not even going to get one word. "Sorry if I was rude last night. I was feeling a little out of sorts."

She shrugged as though it didn't matter whether he was rude or not.

"This is really good."

"Thanks."

She obviously thought that fixing his breakfast was no big deal, and perhaps she was right. This was simply another example of her ability to remember preferences and follow directions. It didn't mean she cared anything about him.

Ben almost wished Jackie had been there. Terri would at least talk to *her.* Of course, Jackie would never ask the right questions.

Terri cleaned her plate and then gathered up the dishes and carried them into the kitchen. Ben moved to the couch and turned on the television, figuring she'd toss the plates in the dishwasher and then join him. By the time he realized she was washing them by hand, proving that she'd rather wash dishes than sit with him and watch some show about sport fishing, he had no idea what to do or say to her. But when she poured another cup of coffee for him and left the room, he realized why he was feeling so bugged by it all.

She's acting like a servant.

Ben had no idea how long he sat there in stunned silence, but he heard her door close very gently. Either she didn't want to talk to him or didn't want to disturb him. Ultimately, it didn't matter because the message was the same and he heard it, loud and clear. She didn't intend to spend another day with him.

Chapter 8

Having made it through a breakfast that felt more awkward than the previous day's, all Terri could think about was getting out of there. Ben had been much quieter, which could've meant anything, but the way he'd stood silently watching her while she was cooking made her feel very strange. She should have been pleased that he hadn't felt the need to chatter through all her long silences, but then she remembered what he'd said to her the night before. "Go," he'd said. *"Now."*

As if she could forget. She'd never been dismissed quite so effectively before. Not even by Jacqueline. Just thinking about it was every bit as painful as the original experience, building to a climax and ending with a chilling wave that swept over her. She had to stop this somehow before it killed her.

Her attitude was ridiculous and melodramatic—and she knew it—but she couldn't help the way she felt. Again, she could almost hear Constance saying, "He's just a *guy*" the way she'd said it at least a hundred times. *Just a guy.* Just the one—the *only* one—Terri had ever felt anything for in all her twenty-eight years.

Still, she wasn't all *that* old. People were free to fall in love at any age. She'd seen it happen before. The hot-dog vendor had fallen in love with the owner of the little antique store she passed by every day, and they were both in their sixties. That sort of thing happened all the time. Most people her age were long past the stage of first love. She was a grown woman, not a lovesick teenager, and should know better than to let something so trivial have such a profound effect. She should get over it and go on—maybe even go back to the beach and find Shorty and Slim and...*what?* Nothing came to mind, but anything was bound to be better than her current predicament.

Changing quickly into the bikini and then putting a T-shirt and shorts over it, she dropped her key into her beach bag along with some cash and a few other essentials and headed out. With the whole day ahead of her, she decided to go shopping for a hat or a big umbrella along with a novel to read. If she went farther down the beach, Ben might not find her, and she could avoid him—which was exactly what she wanted to do. Avoid him.

She hadn't gone far when she ran across a little boutique and found a big, floppy hat and some clip-on sunglasses. Thinking that Ben might not recognize her if she wore a disguise, she took it a step further, completing her ensemble with a pair of dangling hoop earrings, a beaded necklace, and a colorful batik scrunchy to pull back her hair.

"Not bad," she muttered as she checked out the effect in the mirror. She doubted she would have recognized herself, and Ben barely knew her. What chance did he have?

Then the ultimate, ironic, ignominious thought struck her. She didn't need to hide from him because he probably wouldn't bother to look. With that not-so-cheery thought in mind, all she bought was the hat, the sunglasses, and the scrunchy. Aside from the fact that her ears weren't pierced and the screw-on earrings hurt, jewelry wasn't her thing.

After grabbing some munchies and a couple of bottles of water at another store, she cut between two hotels and went back to the beach. Choosing a spot four hotels to the north, she pulled off her shirt and shorts and spread out her towel. She was sitting there, happily slathering sunscreen on her arms when Shorty and Slim walked by. It was then that she realized that any disguise was pointless as long as she was wearing that frickin' purple bikini.

Their eyes lit up as they spotted her and they strolled over, stopping at the edge of her towel.

"So, did you get all your groceries put away?" Shorty asked.

"Sure did," she replied. "Thanks for your help."

"You're welcome." Hesitating a moment, he went on. "So, your, um, *friend* isn't with you today?"

"No," she said firmly.

"Want some help with that?" Slim asked, indicating the bottle of Coppertone. "I could do your back for you."

Shorty seemed to think this was inordinately funny for some reason. Stifling a laugh, he gave Slim an odd look.

"Sure." She almost said he could do any part of her he liked, but thought better of it and held her tongue. It was precisely the sort of suggestive remark Constance would have made, but it wasn't Terri's style.

Having Slim's hands on her wasn't quite the earth-shattering experience it had been with Ben, but it was nice. He had warm hands and a firm, gentle touch. The sensation was quite pleasant and made her feel almost chatty.

"So, are you two the Boy Scout contingency for this stretch of the beach? Helping little old ladies with their luggage and groceries and such?"

Shorty chuckled. "Sort of. We have a...*thing* we do when we're on vacation together."

This sounded interesting. "Oh? And that would be...?"

"Well, we look for a lady who doesn't seem to be having much fun, and we try to change that."

"Good Samaritans, as it were?" They were already making Terri feel better, and she didn't even have any bags for them to carry.

He nodded. "Something like that."

"And what do you do to help?"

"Oh, lots of things," Shorty replied. "Just about anything, in fact. We take them to lunch or dinner, go parasailing, hang out at the beach, go shopping—stuff like that. Once we even took a lady on a deep-sea fishing trip."

That sounded very nice, but there had to be a catch. "So what do you expect in return?"

He smiled and said nothing more, but Slim spoke up from behind her, his lips mere millimeters from her ear. "It's sort of a fringe benefit for you too," he said softly. "You get the best sex you've ever had in your life. With both of us. Together. At the same time."

Whoa... Of course, being the best would be easy, since in Terri's case it would be the *only*. She wondered if she ought to mention that.

"No strings, no pain, no broken hearts, and no regrets." He smoothed more lotion over her shoulders and down her arms. "Interested?"

Terri cleared her throat, but still sounded strained when she spoke. "What makes you think I'm not having a good time?"

Shorty might not have been the smarter of the two, yet he clearly knew the meaning of skepticism. One raised eyebrow proved he was under no illusion she was having the time of her life.

"Well, okay. You're right about that much," she conceded. "How long have you been doing this?"

"This is our fourth year," Shorty replied. "We started when we turned eighteen."

"And you guys are that good?"

"Well, we don't have any references to hand out," Slim murmured in her ear, "but no one's ever complained—or been disappointed." He dropped a soft, warm kiss just below her earlobe. "They've all seemed very...*pleased.*"

"Well, you guys are awfully cute—"

"Thank you," they replied in unison.

"—but I really shouldn't."

"I'll tell you what," Slim said. "You spend a couple of hours with us—we'll do anything you like—and then you can decide if you want the full package deal or not."

"What does all of this cost me?" She wasn't a shrewd New Yorker for nothing.

"Not a dime," he replied.

Shorty sat down in front of her and reached for her leg, stretching it out in front of her so that she lay back against Slim, who handed him the bottle. "Think of this as a free sample."

She snorted derisively. "You two sound like a couple of con men. I expect you'll rob me blind and then murder me or something."

"We've heard that before," Slim said. "It isn't true at all. We're just here to have a good time and to see to it that you do too."

Shorty began sliding his hand up Terri's leg, coating it with sunscreen. "We don't steal anything. We don't need to."

"Get really big tips, huh?" Her voice sounded strange, probably because she'd never been touched in quite that way before. Ben had confined himself to working on her back.

Shorty shook his head slowly. "What we want from you won't cost you anything, but if it makes you feel better, you can pay your share of the expenses."

"But you don't have to," Slim added quickly. "We've got plenty of money saved up." He moved back and carefully repositioned her so that her head was resting in his lap. "We also get tested for every disease you can think of—documentation available upon request. Plus, we use condoms—with spermicide—faithfully. You won't get pregnant and you won't get sick."

Terri opened one eye and peered up at him. "Guaranteed?"

"Well, nothing's a hundred percent certain."

"I know," she muttered. "Just checking."

Slim steadily massaged her upper chest and then moved farther down across her stomach while Shorty worked on her inner thighs. Their hands were warm, touching her in a way that was intimate, and yet innocent enough for a public beach.

Her breath caught in her throat more than once but somehow she still managed a question. "So, how did you get started doing this? It seems a little…unusual."

"Mostly by accident the first time," Slim replied. "It just sort of turned out that way. After that, we made a point of it."

"Yeah, the first time was awesome!" Shorty exclaimed. "She was forty years old, and we had the best time with her. I'll never forget that summer if I live to be a hundred."

"She taught us how to do things I'd never even heard of before." Slim's voice contained a touch of awe, mingled with respect. "She was…*wonderful.*"

"So, are your…*ladies* always older than you guys?"

"Well, so far they have been," Slim said. "But I'm guessing you aren't much older than we are."

"I'm twenty-eight, but there's something else you should know about me. I've never…*done* that."

"Been with two guys? Don't worry, none of the others had either. Well, except that first one. We'll show you how."

"No, that's not what I meant," she said carefully. "I mean *ever.* With anyone."

Shorty gasped. "No shit? You're a virgin?"

She nodded, although given just how far his hand had reached between her thighs, it may or may not have been true at the time. Another inch or two and he'd be there.

The two men exchanged another meaningful glance.

"Oh, wow!" Slim whispered fervently. "Can we be first, please? We won't hurt you, I promise. We'll be real careful."

Shorty chuckled. "Yeah, Chris is just about the most patient guy I've ever seen. Which is a good thing, considering."

Terri was almost afraid to hear the reply, but she just *had* to ask. "Considering *what?*"

"Considering that he's one of those guys who likes going in through the back door."

Terri might have been a virgin, but she knew what he was talking about. She wasn't stupid, and she had ears. She looked up at Slim/Chris, who was grinning sheepishly. "Really?"

"Oh, yeah," he said. "Joey loves watching me do it too."

Terri rolled her eyes. "I'll just bet you do."

"No," Joey/Shorty said quickly. "That's not what he meant. He means that I love seeing the look on a woman's face when he does it. I can see how good it feels to them and how amazed they are that it does."

"It's one of the things that first lady taught me," Chris said. "She wanted us both, and she showed us how. I liked it that way."

"Yeah, and they're always facing me," Joey said, "so I get to see the 'look.' It's almost better than—well, maybe not better than actually doing it, but it's still really cool."

If she'd suspected that these guys were con artists or meant anyone any harm, the more they talked, the more obvious it became that they were nothing of the kind. Unless they were extremely good actors, which she doubted. They seemed quite genuine, and very sweet, really. Terri was just about to throw caution to the wind and agree to their proposal when a shadow fell across her face.

Another ten minutes—maybe even five—and she'd have been gone. But noooo. Ben just *had* to catch her lying on the beach with two guys who had their hands all over her. And that damned flowery purple bikini was there to advertise the fact that it was Terri they were working on. Chris even had his fingers under the edge of the top half.

"What the hell do you think you're doing?" Ben demanded.

Terri wasn't sure if he was talking to Chris and Joey or to her, but she opted to respond anyway. "Sunbathing."

"Well, you might have at least *mentioned* that you were going out," he said. "I've been all over the place trying to find you."

"Sorry."

"That's all you have to say? Sorry?"

"Uh-huh."

Terri thought he might have been intimidating enough to scare the guys away, but they stood their ground. In fact, they didn't even stop what they were doing, which clearly irritated Ben. "Will you two get your filthy hands off her?"

Joey raised a hand and examined it carefully. "They look clean enough to me."

"Are you her father?" Chris sounded so innocent Terri almost believed he didn't know the truth. *Maybe he's a better actor than I thought.*

Ben's face registered the insult and Terri waited for the explosion.

With a visible effort, he bit back a retort and waited a second or two before he spoke. "No, I'm not her *father*. But, Terri, will you please tell me where you're going the next time?"

Two could play that game. "Sure. And exactly where will *you* be?"

"Over by the pool."

Stretching her arms, Terri let out what she hoped was a contented sigh. "Sounds good. I'll see you later, then."

It was clearly a dismissal, but he took it well, simply nodding and walking away.

"He's got the hots for you," Chris said as soon as Ben was out of earshot. "You know that, don't you?"

Terri shook her head. "No, he doesn't, and he's got a perfectly beautiful wife. I don't think she loves him, but—"

"I'm not kidding," Chris said earnestly. "That was a territorial skirmish if I ever saw one. I'm surprised he didn't kick sand in my face. He only backed down because he knew he didn't have a legitimate claim on you."

Which seemed an odd way for a twenty-two-year-old beach stud to be putting it. "You seem awfully smart. What are you, an anthropologist?"

Joey rolled his eyes. "He's still in college, but he's always saying things like that."

"Anthropology major," Chris said. "I find it extremely fascinating."

Terri glanced up to see if the signature raised eyebrow accompanied his Mr. Spock-like comment.

It didn't. All she saw was an expectant smile.

"So, did you enjoy the free sample?" Once again, his fingers swept enticingly beneath the fabric of her bikini top. "Would you like more?"

Terri could hear it now. *She was out screwing around with a couple of beach boys all day long,* Ben would tell Jacqueline. *She ignored me just the way you do.* Which of course he would never actually say. Terri knew she was being a bit hateful, but at the moment, she felt it was justified.

"Let me think about it for a while," she said. "I'll probably be around here all day. Ask me again later."

"Okay," Chris said, but his smile never wavered.

Mr. Anthropology Major knew he had her, all right. She was going to say yes. She just couldn't say it *yet.*

Of course, he probably knew that, too

Chapter 9

Ben went back to the pool feeling about a thousand years old. *Are you her father?* That crack cut him deeper than he would've thought. Still, those college boys were a lot younger than Terri. She had to be somewhere in her late twenties—maybe even thirty. Okay, so maybe she *was* closer to their age than she was to his, but women liked older men, didn't they?

Doesn't matter if they do or they don't. You're a married man, and she isn't interested in you. She's made that very plain.

While that sounded like excellent advice, it didn't make him feel any better. He had absolutely no right to question anything Terri did. She wasn't his wife. She wasn't even his assistant. So why did he want to beat the living shit out of those boys?

She was younger than him, inexperienced and vulnerable. It was natural for him to feel protective of her.

Wasn't it?

If that was all he felt, it might be different. But his feelings weren't the least bit fatherly. Nor were they like that of an older brother. No, his feelings were more…predatory, possessive, and, yes, protective—feelings he shouldn't have been having toward her or any woman other than his wife.

This farce was already making him crazy, and that was before Jackie told him to sleep in the other bed in Terri's room like it was no big deal. What the hell did she think he was? A fuckin' eunuch?

No, she knew better than that. Jackie's opinion of him ran more along the lines of a stag in rut—though he'd seldom had the opportunity to display those tendencies. Far more likely was that she believed Terri had no sex appeal whatsoever, and that even a man who hadn't had sex in over a year wouldn't be tempted by her. Ben wasn't sure which part of that ticked him off more. Besides, he had news for Jackie. Terri had plenty of sex appeal, even when she was wearing her all-concealing robe, and especially when she was wearing that purple bikini.

Ben still couldn't quite reconcile himself with the overwhelming surge of jealousy he'd felt when he'd spotted Terri being caressed by those two boys. He couldn't recall ever having felt anything like it before—*ever*—which was unsettling, to say the least.

He was beginning to wish he'd never come here, and if he had any sense at all, he would leave now, before he did something *really* stupid.

∞CR

Terri was feeling a little guilty, despite the fact that she hadn't done anything wrong. And Ben hadn't either. He'd simply made it impossible for her to sleep in the living room and had been looking out for her. She should be grateful. She should have left Chris and Joey and gone back to spend another day on the beach with Ben. However, having been the recipient of more male attention than she'd ever had in her life, she still didn't quite know what to make of it. Deciding that it might be best if she stayed away from all of them for an hour or so, she lay out on the sand for a while, swam in the ocean a bit, and then, deciding she'd had enough sun for one day, went back to the hotel pool, which was sheltered beneath the building, along with the hot tub and a lazy river.

She didn't see Ben at first, so she chose a chaise lounge at random and dumped her beach bag on it. Deciding on the lazy river instead of the pool, she selected a big, doughnut-shaped float from the pile by the steps, got in the water, and paddled around for a while. She was drifting peacefully on the current when Ben caught up with her.

"Lose your new friends?" His innocent tone didn't fool her.

Underneath it, he sounded pleased.

"No."

"Where are they, then?"

"Oh, I'm sure they're around here somewhere." *Hopefully watching this exchange and feeling possessive and jealous themselves.* Having three men vying for her attention was a new and admittedly heady experience for Terri. Perhaps if she'd gotten out more and done something in her life besides eat, breathe, sleep, work, and get hooked on sci-fi, the whole male-female mating dance might have been old hat, but as things stood, it wasn't—and she was enjoying every minute of it.

"That was a rather disgusting display out there on the beach," he said. "I'm surprised at you."

"Sorry to disappoint." She almost added, *Dad!* but figured he'd retaliate by knocking her off her float. Being quite comfortable, she wasn't in the mood for horseplay.

Ben scowled, clearly miffed at not having gotten a rise out of her. He was quiet for a while after that, and when he did speak again, he changed the subject. "Did Jackie say anything to you this morning?"

"No." *Although she probably should have.* After all, Terri had shared a room with her husband. If their situations had been reversed, Terri would have had *plenty* to say about it—for once—but then, if she'd been in Jacqueline's place, there would have been no need. Ben would have been in bed with Terri where he belonged, and Jacqueline wouldn't have gotten within thirty feet of him.

"You didn't see her, or she didn't say anything?"

"Both."

"Mind telling me why you just up and disappeared like that?"

"I needed to get out. Alone."

"Oh, so you like your solitude, huh?"

"Mm-hm."

"Why is that?"

"I don't have to talk if I'm by myself."

"Why is talking such a hard thing for you?"

"Don't know," she said with a shrug. "Just is."

"You didn't seem to have any trouble talking to those boys." His tone was casual, but still held an undercurrent of pique.

"They did most of the talking."

"You *do* know what they're after, don't you? They're just looking to get laid."

"Mm-hm." That might have been the gist of it, but considering the way they'd made the offer, Terri really didn't have a problem with that.

"Their kind doesn't want anything else," he went on. "They're just out to take anything they can get."

"Mm-hm." Constance's voice sounded in Terri's head. *They have penises. Don't trust them.*

Ben seemed to back down slightly. "Well, just so you know that."

Terri nodded. Of course, not trusting a penis didn't necessarily mean it wouldn't feel good. Then she realized that she *wanted* to get laid, and if she couldn't have her boss's husband, whom she should have known better than to fall for to begin with, she wanted to get laid by those two sweet, adorable beach boys from North Carolina. Both of them. Together. At the same time...

Sitting up, Terri spotted them almost immediately. They were in the hot tub—watching, waiting. They waved back when she smiled at them, and Chris gave her a questioning look, gesturing back and forth between them. With her confirming nod, he nudged Joey. Grinning broadly, they bailed out of the tub and came across the patio to the lazy river. Ben had drifted farther on, and Terri doubted that he even heard the soft splash she made as she slipped off her float. She swam over to the steps and her two beach boys reached down to help her out of the water. Both of them. Together. At the same time...

Joey scurried over to retrieve her beach bag, and then caught up with Terri and Chris. Ben had drifted past the bend in the river, out of sight.

Joey slipped an arm around her waist. "Want some lunch first?"

Terri nodded. She wasn't sure whether sex was better on an empty stomach or a full one, but she was starving.

"What would you like?"

"Chris and Joey," she said promptly. "With all the trimmings— and maybe a sandwich on the side. Oh, and just in case you're interested, my name is Terri."

"We know," Chris said. "We pay attention to details." Smiling, he wrapped his arm around her shoulders and pulled her up close. His lips brushed her cheek, sending a thrill racing over her skin. "And we don't miss much, either."

"We're going to have a Terri sandwich," Joey chuckled. "But you probably need some real food."

"We've got some stuff in our fridge," Chris said. "Not a lot, but I promise you won't go hungry. You can have anything you want."

"Crab? Lobster? Shrimp?" she teased. "Got that?"

"No, but we can get just about anything delivered—or we can take you out for lunch."

"You'd do that?" She was surprised that he would be willing to delay his gratification for so long. "I mean, going out would take longer."

Chris grinned. "I'm very patient. Remember?"

"Yes, I remember." She elbowed him in the ribs. "You're not the only one with a good memory." Out of all those stored up memories, nothing thus far could compare with the way it felt to be walking to the elevator flanked by two hot, handsome young men while she wore nothing but that little purple bikini.

Joey summoned the elevator and Chris pulled her even closer. Kissing the top of her head, he murmured, "You won't regret this. I promise."

"I'd better not," she warned. "I'll sic Ben on you if you don't get it right."

He grinned. "You won't have to do that. We'll keep on until

you're satisfied with the results."
   Holy shit.

Chapter 10

Terri half expected them to pounce on her in the elevator. But like Chris said, they were patient fellows. She wasn't the least bit patient herself, and she didn't wait for lunch delivery, either. As they ushered her into their room and she saw that there was only one king-size bed, she opted for a peanut butter and jelly sandwich and a glass of cranberry juice, which, aside from a six pack of Budweiser, was all they had.

"We don't cook much," Joey admitted with a shrug. "And we didn't know what you'd like."

"Are you saying you'd stock your fridge with whatever I asked for?"

"Oh, sure," he said, nodding. "We always do that."

"So, if I asked for caviar and champagne, you'd get it for me?"

Chris nodded and bit into his sandwich.

"If we knew where to get it, that is," Joey said, turning to Chris. "Remember Sherry? She wanted some strange stuff we'd never even heard of, but we found it. What was that, anyway?"

"Hummus," Chris replied. "Some kind of bean dip. Anyway, we got it for her. She seemed pleased."

Terri couldn't imagine why anyone would even be thinking about hummus when these two were hanging around, but there was no accounting for taste.

"What would you like us to get for you?" Joey asked.

Terri thought for a moment. "Jalapeño poppers from Arby's with ranch dressing and lots of salt."

"Well, you're easy," Chris said with a chuckle. "I think we can manage that."

This marked the second time in the past day or so that a man had said that to her, but she let it pass. "I just *love* jalapeños. I think I could eat those poppers 'til they were coming out my ears."

"Well, just so you don't suck my dick right afterwards." Chris shuddered. "I think that would hurt."

"Hadn't thought of that, but then, I've never sucked anyone's dick before." She couldn't recall having ever said that, either. These guys were making her downright talkative—and sexual talk, no less.

"Well, you can try it and see if you like it," he said reasonably. "Some girls don't, you know. That Sherry we were talking about couldn't even stand the thought of it."

"Do *you* like it?" Terri had never had such strange conversation before, and found it oddly exciting.

"Having my cock sucked?" Chris asked with surprise. "Are you kidding? I doubt if there's ever been a man alive on this earth who didn't."

And the anthropology major would know all about that. "So you both do?"

"Oh, yeah!" Joey said. "And having my balls sucked is like…heaven."

"But not after eating jalapeños, right?"

He paused, obviously giving this question careful consideration. "You know, I might even like that. Never tried it, but—"

"Not me," Chris said firmly. "No jalapeños."

Considering Chris's other preference, Terri wasn't sure she wanted his penis to have any added spice to it, either. She had an idea it might come back to bite her in the butt. Having thought that, it was a good five minutes before she could stop laughing long enough to tell them what was so funny.

"You see!" Chris exclaimed. "I *told* you it was a bad idea!" Of course, he then went on to inform Terri that it really wouldn't matter since he would be using a condom, but she promised not to pepper his dick, just the same.

The ensuing silence drew attention to the fact that they had all finished lunch and the guys were clearly waiting for her do or say something. She took a deep breath. "So, what now?"

"Whatever you want," they replied in unison.

"Well," she said hesitantly. "I should probably take a shower before I do anything."

This suggestion drew huge smiles from both men, and Chris nodded his approval. "Excellent choice! Ever take a shower with two guys before?"

Terri blinked. That wasn't exactly what she'd had in mind. She'd never taken a shower with *one* man, let alone two, and she wasn't sure she wanted to start. Not yet, anyway. "If it's all the same to you, I believe I'd rather do it alone."

Their smiles vanished.

"Oh, but it's really fun!" Joey protested. "We get you between us and soap you up and wash you all over and—"

Remembering how good their hands had felt when they were slathering sunscreen on her, she waved her arms for silence. "Okay, okay! You sold me. Just don't spoil the surprise. Look, I've hardly ever even had *lunch* with many men before. You two go ahead and do whatever you consider to be appropriate. This is a learning experience for me. Teach me whatever you think I should know."

"Okay then," Chris said. "Lesson number two: sex is fun, feels good, and you don't have to do anything you don't want to—but you should be willing to give everything a try, at least once."

"Don't knock it 'til you've tried it?"

"Exactly."

Terri frowned. "What was lesson number one? Did I miss it?"

"No, lesson number one was to drink lots of cranberry juice so you won't get a bladder infection, which can be a problem when you're having lots of sex—you know…Honeymoon Cystitis? But you drank it already, so I didn't mention it."

Terri's gaze darted back and forth between the two men. "You guys have obviously put a lot of thought into this."

"Well, we promised you wouldn't get sick," Chris reminded

her. "That's one way of preventing such things. Nothing will stop this whole thing quicker than a bladder infection—unless it's a yeast infection. We're very careful about that, too."

Terri couldn't help but chuckle. "You guys crack me up. I think I've fallen in with a couple of—well, I'm not sure *what* I've fallen into here, but it's certainly different. I doubt that I've ever had such a frank discussion before—not even with my friend Constance, and believe me, she's done it *all.*"

Then she realized that the one thing Constance had never mentioned was having been part of a threesome. If things went as planned, Terri would have a story that would top anything Constance had ever told her—though she would *never* believe it.

As though reading her thoughts, Chris's lips curled into a devilish grin. "You'll have a better story now, won't you?"

Terri nodded decisively. "Okay, then. A shower it is."

Joey took her hand and the next thing she knew, Terri was in a big, oval tub with two men. Two fully aroused, *naked* men, which was something she'd never even *seen* before—at least, not up close and personal. She'd seen pictures, but the reality was breathtaking. She was surprised she didn't up and faint on them, but fascination overrode the shock factor.

Chris and Joey had her break the ice by washing them first, which was another new experience for Terri, and one that they all seemed to enjoy. She quickly discovered that she liked the feel of a warm, hard penis in her hand, and if their reactions were anything to go by, the guys liked it too. She found the sharp contrast between the hard strength of their cocks and the soft scrotal folds encasing their firm testicles quite remarkable. Both felt oddly foreign—as unique and intriguing as putting her hands on an exotic animal—not like something that was part of a human being at all. This wasn't too surprising since Terri had always thought of men as another species entirely.

Once she had the guys squeaky clean, they started in on her. Terri was still wearing her bikini, but it wasn't long before Chris and

Joey removed it. Chris worked on the back while Joey did the front, massaging her breasts and bottom at the same time. She was okay with that—it felt very nice and wasn't too intense—but when Joey reached between her legs, similar to the way he had on the beach, she got a little weak in the knees.

"You guys," she said faintly, "I feel sort of…weird."

"Here," Joey said, pulling her up close to him. "Just put your arms around my neck. I won't let you fall." Joey was just a smidgen shorter than Terri, and his soapy penis slid between her legs very nicely, somewhat like straddling a fence rail. She wasn't sure a penis would hold her up quite as effectively, but it was just about as thick. He leaned closer to whisper in her ear. "Doesn't that feel good?"

About all Terri could do was nod, because he was right, it *did* feel good. He was warm and slick and her entire body was pressed up against him. She buried her face in the side of his neck, and a moment later a fully-lathered Chris was pressed tightly against her backside. He was taller than she, and his penis nestled comfortably in the small of her back. This was lovely, but when he spread his feet apart and slid his penis into the cleft of her buttocks and over her anus, she let out an involuntary gasp.

As he teased her opening with the head of his cock, his warm breath tickled her ear, sending tingles racing down her spine. "D'you like that, Terri?"

Her reply was a barely audible moan.

"I think that was a yes," Joey said. "Keep going."

Terri didn't think she could take much more, but Chris kept on until all of a sudden, her stomach muscles contracted and she recoiled as if she'd been punched in the belly. Only it felt a helluva lot better than being punched. She lurched forward, gasping against Joey's chest.

"Whoa!" Joey exclaimed exultantly. "Orgasm number one!"

"Well, that was quick," Chris remarked. "See, I told you she'd be a good one. Was I right, or was I *right?"*

"You were *absolutely* right," Joey agreed, giving Chris a high five. "She is *totally* hot. Hey, what do you say we rinse her off and get her out of here?"

"Yeah," Chris agreed. "I think she needs to lie down for a while."

Terri felt like a wet rag and didn't give a shit that they were talking about her as though she'd actually been one.

Chris pried her off of Joey and pulled her under the spray of warm water. "You okay, baby?"

She nodded without uttering a sound as he tipped her chin up and kissed her—which was also a first. It wasn't a quick little peck, either. He *really* kissed her, delving past her parted lips to taste her fully. A moment later she felt that same quivering sensation deep inside and waited for the impact. This time she couldn't fall forward and her knee snapped up instead, fortunately to the *outside* of his leg, or she would've hit him in the balls.

"Holy shit!" Joey exclaimed. "That's amazing! Here, let me try."

Chris broke off the kiss, taking a deep breath. "I think she likes me," he said a little smugly. "Maybe she won't do it for you."

"Well, I'm gonna find out," Joey insisted. "C'mere, Terri. Kiss me."

Joey took her in his arms, his tongue sliding past her lips while his thick penis pushed between her thighs. She had a little more presence of mind this time and kissed him back, thrusting her own tongue against his as he pumped his cock between her legs. She must've liked him just as much as she liked Chris because it took less than ten seconds before another climax hit her.

Joey drew back with a satisfied smirk, but never stopped the movement of his hips. "See, she likes me, too."

"What's not to like?" Terri muttered. "You're both adorable."

"And so are you." Joey wrapped his arms around the small of her back and pulled her up close. "You're wet, too. I can feel it."

Terri might have been a bit groggy, but this seemed fairly obvious. "Well, *duh*. I'm in the shower."

"Not *that* kind of wet," he said with a slow shake of his head. *"This* kind." Reaching down, he slid a finger past his cock and up inside her. He might have been wet from the water, but this moisture was nearly frictionless, as though he had some sort of lubricant on his skin.

Joey had just gone where no man—even her gynecologist was female—had been before, rendering Terri momentarily speechless as delicious waves of pleasure rose from his touch—warm, soothing, and amazingly slick. "You've got shampoo or soap on your finger, don't you?"

He shook his head, a knowing smile on his lips. "No, Terri. That's coming from *you.*"

"Well, s—so what?" she sputtered.

"It means you're ready to fuck." Chris sounded quite sure of himself. *"Very* ready."

"Oh," she said blankly. It seemed reasonable, but what the hell did she know about such things?

He nodded toward the bedroom. "Let's go. Grab some towels, Joey."

"Hey, shouldn't we dry her hair first?"

Chris examined her hair carefully. "Yeah, we wouldn't want her to catch cold. That would be bad."

After helping Terri out of the tub, Chris dried her hair with the hotel hair dryer while Joey dried off the rest of her, then himself, and then Chris, as well, which Terri thought was sort of interesting. Constance once had a boyfriend whom she'd said was bisexual. Maybe these guys were too, although it might have been just to speed things up. Terri didn't ask.

The reason she didn't ask was because her hair wasn't completely dry yet, and, in the meantime, Joey occupied himself by licking her nipples until she had another orgasm. Was there was an upper limit on the number of orgasms a woman could have, or was her body simply using up its quota from the time she'd reached puberty until now? Either way, she figured it would probably slack off after a while. For the time being though, she was enjoying every single one of them.

Chris finished drying her hair and then began kissing her on the neck, moving lower and lower until he was also kissing a nipple. Under this dual assault on her senses, her knees gave way completely, but the two of them managed to catch her before she hit the floor. They carried her into the other room, laying her carefully on the bed.

They'd said she was ready to fuck, yet they still didn't do it right away. Joey began kissing her again while Chris nudged her legs apart. *Okay. Here we go, he's going to do it now.*

But Chris was a patient fellow. Apparently deciding that Terri required further preparation, he began licking her, evoking even more previously unknown sensations from her body. Her mind might not have known how to react to any of it, but her body certainly did; it had only been waiting until her brain figured out what she'd been missing all those years. She knew she had a clitoris and knew it was supposed to be sensitive, but it had always seemed to her to be a rather superfluous organ, much like her appendix. She knew better now. With it, he was taking her somewhere she'd never been before and had never even dreamed of going. Intense, overwhelming and— *whoa, shit!* What the guys had referred to before as an orgasm was *nothing* compared to what happened this time. She was reminded of the way the Death Star exploded at the end of *Star Wars,* only this was even more spectacular. She could almost hear Han Solo shouting, *"Great shot, kid! That was one in a million!"*

Or perhaps Joey said it to Chris. She wasn't completely sure about that.

Chris backed off and Joey crawled up over her, cradling her shoulders in his arms and kissing her deeply. Although her mind was still reeling from her orgasm, she was vaguely aware of the sound of a package being ripped open. It took her another moment to realize that Chris was putting a condom on Joey. He had to be, because Joey never stopped kissing her, and he was still holding her with both arms when Chris slapped Joey on the butt. "Go for it, big guy!"

Nudging her legs farther apart as he moved closer, Joey pressed his cockhead against her entrance while Chris took hold of her ankles, raising her legs up even higher. Terri knew just exactly how thick Joey's cock was, and was feeling a bit apprehensive when, with just a slight pang, he slid right in. Her eyes flew open in surprise, and she nearly choked on the sharp intake of air into her lungs.

Joey smoothed a hand over her hair. "Okay, baby?"

"Yeah," she replied breathlessly. "I think so."

"Doesn't hurt, does it?"

"Well, maybe just a little," she admitted. "But not too much."

"You tell me if you want me to stop or slow down or whatever, okay?"

"Mm-hm," she replied, nodding vigorously.

"Okay then, here goes."

With that, he began moving, sliding that big cock in and out of her like a piston. Slowly at first and then with increasing speed and depth, he plunged into her. Everything about it felt fabulous. His penis inside her, his balls tickling her bottom, her legs pressed against his warm body—there wasn't any part of it she didn't like.

Until he slowed down and stopped. She let out a groan. "Oh, please don't stop. That feels *so* good."

"But it'll be even better in a minute," he said. "Just hold on."

Terri didn't know how he did it, but a second or two later, he flipped them both over so that she sat on top of him, straddling him like a horse. When he spread his legs apart, Chris came up from behind and put his hands on her shoulders, whispering in her ear. "Get settled on him good and then lean forward."

She did as he instructed and lay face down on Joey's chest. She felt something cold and wet on her backside and then what was probably his finger, probing her very gently, teasing the opening until she relaxed enough to admit him. She was nervous but had to admit it felt fabulous. Pretty soon he had her moaning even more than Joey had.

More cold, wet fluid and then something much larger took the place of his finger. With a slight push forward, and then back, over and over again, he worked with her. Never going in too far, just a push, a stretch and then out. This went on for several minutes, and then something else happened. Something let go, gave way, or relaxed, Terri wasn't sure which.

"Okay, Joey," Chris said. *"Now."*

Joey took Terri's head in his hands and aimed her face toward his own. "Look at me, Terri."

And then Chris came in all the way.

As facial expressions go, hers must've been a dilly. Her jaw dropped and her eyes felt like they were about to pop out of her head.

A huge grin spread across Joey's face. "Oh, *yeah!* That has to be the best ever!"

"Breathe, Terri," Chris urged. "Don't hold your breath."

On his command, Terri let out her pent-up breath and then took another. What he was doing didn't hurt, but the sensation was so overwhelming she couldn't even think straight.

"Come on," he urged, rubbing her back. "Relax and keep breathing. That's it. In and out. In and out. Good girl, keep going. Ready, Joey?"

"You bet."

"Okay, then. One, two, three… *go."*

With both of them moving inside her, it wasn't long before Terri was making sounds she'd never even *heard* before, let alone made herself. Her eyes filled with tears and her moans became sobs as she experienced the most intense pleasure of her life. Grabbing Joey by the shoulders, she held on for dear life.

He threaded his fingers through her hair. "Still okay?"

What came out of her mouth was more of a whimper than a word, but she did manage to nod. They kept on moving, sometimes in unison, sometimes with a see-saw effect until her body was one quivering mass of ecstasy and she was crying out with each breath. Suddenly, her mind went completely blank and the Death Star exploded again, only this time it was more like the Special Edition version. Her climactic scream nearly drowned out Joey's, but she could feel him stiffen beneath her as he drove his cock into her with one last powerful thrust.

Joey had already relaxed completely when Chris clutched her hips, making an inarticulate sound as he rammed into her even farther than before. He held her there for a few breathless moments, and then let go, gradually ramping down his speed until he finally stopped altogether.

Terri was barely aware of them as they both withdrew very carefully from her body. One of them wiped her off with a towel, but she had no idea who it was. Rolling over onto her side, she felt so helplessly weak she couldn't have gotten out of bed if the hotel had been on fire.

"Here, sweetheart," Chris said, holding her up in his arms. "Drink this."

She took a sip. *Cranberry juice.* After a bit, he made sure she got up to use the potty. When she came back to bed, the guys snuggled up on either side of her and Joey pulled the sheet up over them. Apparently she was in good hands, which was a good thing because she wanted to do it again, and again, and again…

Chapter 11

Terri awoke to the sound of crunching and the unmistakable aroma of jalapeños. Opening her eyes, she saw Chris lying next to her with a bag of potato chips on his chest.

He aimed the bag toward her. "These aren't poppers, but it was the best I could do at the store across the street."

She reached into the bag and pulled out a chip. "I bet they don't have champagne and caviar, either."

"You're probably right." He paused for a moment, eying her curiously. "So, how was it? The sex, I mean. Was it okay?"

Okay? That description seemed inadequate, somehow—like referring to the Boston Marathon as a leisurely stroll through the park. Terri munched on a chip, savoring the peppery flavor while contemplating her reply.

"You know something, Chris?" Joey piped up from behind her. "You should try actually *facing* a woman when you fuck her. Then you wouldn't have to ask that question."

"Yeah, well, when we're doing this together, that's about the only way I *can* do it," Chris argued. "It's not like I do it that way all the time."

"Well, just don't expect me to ever switch positions," Joey said. "I'd kill her." He leaned closer to Terri. "No one's ever asked me to, either. I've been referred to as The Coke Can."

Knowing just how apt this nickname was, Terri didn't argue the point. Chris's cock was longer and a bit slimmer. No, Joey was fine staying right where he was.

Chris gave her a nudge. "So? What did you think?"

Terri studiously selected another chip from the bag and licked the salt off it before she replied. "Not so sure of yourself now, are you?" His anxious expression drew a small chuckle. "Don't worry. I liked it just fine."

"Fine?" he echoed. *"Fine? That's all?"*

Joey cackled with laughter and punched Chris in the arm. "Oh, shut up, Chris. She loved it."

"Yes, I did, and I promise to do it again sometime." She paused, squinting at the clock. "But right now, I'm starving and I want more than potato chips."

Chris ran a finger between her bare breasts, making her nipples tingle. "Well, unless you want us to order a pizza, you might want to go back to your room for something to wear. Or does dear old Dad expect you home for dinner?"

Terri frowned. "I'm not sure. Jacqueline is having dinner at the conference, but I don't know about Ben. And for the record, he's not my *dad*, and he isn't all that old, either. He's just …well, I don't know, exactly. All I know is that he's the first man I ever had any…feelings for."

Joey reached across for a handful of chips, brushing her breasts with his arm. "This Jacqueline is your boss and Ben is her husband, right?"

So this is what it's like after you have sex with someone. Interesting... She nodded, trying not to overreact to the casual, yet intimate contact. "Yes, and it makes things a little…strange."

Joey's description was more graphic. "Actually, it sucks big ones."

"I suppose it does."

"But he likes you," Chris insisted. "Maybe they'll get a divorce."

"I doubt that. I mean, I only met him yesterday morning."

"But you like him, don't you?"

"I'm not sure. It was the strangest thing. I was sitting there at the airport, and he was laughing at something this kid said to him, and when he looked up, our eyes met and I…*felt* something."

Considering the subsequent events, she might have to rethink that that little bout of chest pain. Her experiences with Ben hadn't been all hearts and flowers, so maybe Cupid didn't shoot her after all. A severe case of indigestion or even a heart attack was more likely.

Chris touched the center of her chest. "Right here, wasn't it?"

Terri's reluctant nod apparently confirmed his suspicions.

"He must have felt it too because he didn't like it one little bit when he found us with you on the beach."

She shook her head. "I doubt it. He might feel responsible for me in some way, but all we've done is argue. I still don't think—" She broke off there as she recalled that idyllic space of time they'd spent together on the beach. From her current perspective, it might have been an excerpt from another life; a life that could have been, not something that had truly happened at all. "There *have* been times we've gotten along just fine, but—"

"It might have been the bikini," Joey suggested. "It certainly got our attention."

"Yeah, right," Terri said with a snort. "Like there aren't a hundred others just like it out there on the beach. I mean, *I've* never worn anything like it before, but lots of other women do."

Joey quirked an eyebrow. "Well, maybe, but—"

Joey might have been skeptical, but Chris pounced on that juicy little tidbit without hesitation. "You've never worn a bikini before? What made you start now?"

"He did," Terri replied.

"Oh, so you got it in an attempt to impress him?"

"No, I bought it because he said if I didn't buy it, he would, and I couldn't let him do that. It just didn't seem right." She took a deep breath and gave them the rest of the story. "He picked it out, insisted that I try it on, and then insisted that I buy it."

Chris and Joey exchanged a very meaningful look.

Joey let out a low whistle. "Baby, he wants you, and he wants you *bad."*

"Oh, he does not!" Terri protested. "Nobody does. You know,

there's a reason I'm an old maid. I've never even dated anyone."

Chris and Joey both burst out laughing.

"Just so you know, we pick women who look like they aren't having any fun," Chris said when he'd recovered enough to speak. "Not women no one would want."

"Well, you should," Terri said firmly. "It's more democratic."

Chris shook his head. "Sorry. It doesn't work that way."

"I suppose not." Sighing, she helped herself to another chip. "I'm probably just as bad. After all, you guys are both adorable, but the thing is…I'd never even *looked* at men before yesterday. I just didn't get it, you know?"

"But you do now, don't you?"

"I guess I do."

The question was, would she ever get it again? And would she even *want* to? Especially since after twenty-eight years of no men at all, she'd managed to team up with two no-strings Romeos and had the hots—or something else entirely, something almost frightening—for a man who was married to her boss. Her choices were questionable at best.

Actually, questionable wasn't the word for it.

Her choices *sucked.*

Big ones.

ଫୀଓ

The one thing Terri hadn't considered when she ran off with Chris and Joey was that at some point, she would have to face Ben. She wasn't looking forward to it—especially since she'd promised to tell him where she was going. If she could have given the guys a key to her room, sent them to get all her stuff, and then moved in with them for the rest of the week, she probably would have done it. Jacqueline might have fired her for deserting her in her hour of need, but at least she wouldn't have Ben fussing at her—and she was pretty sure he would fuss.

Chris had been right about Ben not having a legitimate claim on Terri, but the more she thought about it, the more she realized that he'd behaved as though he at least *thought* he did. Even later on at the pool, he hadn't backed off much, although that was before she'd disappeared on him again. That she'd gone off with Chris and Joey should've been perfectly obvious to anyone, so he shouldn't have been worried. They were nice guys and certainly weren't out to hurt her or anyone else, whether Ben liked the idea or not. They simply wanted to have a good time while they were on vacation, and they weren't married to her boss, which was a major point in their favor. Ben was Jacqueline's husband, whether he chose to act that way or not.

Terri tried to remember all the things Ben had said to her, but not one single word made her think he was going to leave Jacqueline for her, or for anyone else. After all, he'd only come on this trip to talk his wife into having a baby—at least that was what Jacqueline assumed. She might have been mistaken, but either way, the poor guy wasn't having much luck. Now he had *two* women who were trying to avoid him.

In the end, it was Terri's growling stomach that made her brave enough to go back to her room. Having Chris and Joey as escorts helped considerably, but she thought it was strange that everyone seemed to need protection from Ben. His wife had Terri there to keep him from jumping her case, and Terri had her two buddies to make sure he didn't jump hers. She wished their situations had been different. She would've liked him—perhaps even loved him—if he'd been single and if admitting her feelings wouldn't have put her job in jeopardy. Unfortunately, those were two very big *ifs*.

Terri had no idea whether Ben would be in the room or not, and although slipping in quietly to snatch up some clothes would have been the easiest way to avoid a confrontation, she would still have to talk to him sooner or later. She'd already ducked out on him twice, and he obviously didn't care for that tack.

Never having needed to sneak around behind anyone's back

before, Terri was a little surprised at how well she did it, given her lack of practice. *Men.* They could turn perfectly honest women into sneaks. She considered dumping all of them before anything worse happened, but she *did* like them, and having Chris and Joey to talk to made her feel like she had at least two friends in that town. If nothing else, they could take her to the airport if she needed to bolt back to New York.

Having two bodyguards gave Terri the courage to take the direct, honest approach. She would go back to the room, tell Ben she was going out to dinner with the guys, and let the chips fall where they may. Just to prove there were no hard feelings, she might even invite Ben to join them. She'd simply made some new friends. Even *dear old Dad* should be able to deal with that.

Joey slid an arm around her waist. "We should take you out dressed like this. I've never been to dinner with a girl in a purple bikini before. We might get better service."

Chris snorted a laugh. "Only if we have a waiter instead of a waitress."

Terri elbowed Chris in the ribs. "Hush, now. I'm already in enough trouble, and I have no desire to get arrested or thrown out of a restaurant." Inserting the key card in the slot, she pushed open the door and called out for Ben.

Receiving no reply, she checked the bedroom first, deciding it might be best to get dressed before venturing out into the living room. Confronting Ben while wearing the bikini would have been a tactical error, especially if Chris and Joey were with her. She opted to leave them at the end of the hall and braved it alone.

Ben was stretched out on the couch, sound asleep. Even in slumber, there were lines in his face she hadn't noticed before. He looked exhausted, and her heart went out to him. If only she could wake him with a kiss... "Ben?"

He let out a groan and rubbed his eyes. "What time is it?"

"About five thirty. Chris and Joey are taking me out to dinner. Would you like to come with us?"

He opened one eye. "So, *that's* where you've been."

"Well, yeah," she replied. "Where else would I have gone?"

"You didn't have to *go* anywhere. I would have—" He broke off there and turned over on the couch. "Never mind. I believe I'll pass on the dinner invitation. I don't think you need *three* men to take you to dinner."

"I don't need *anyone* to take me to dinner," Terri pointed out. "There are plenty of restaurants within walking distance, and I'm not too particular."

"So I've noticed."

Ben obviously wasn't in a forgiving mood, but she let his sullenness pass and tried to remember if she'd ever been out to dinner with any man who wasn't family or hadn't simply been part of a group she was with. She hadn't—at least, not until now. If she'd been looking for sympathy she could have explained her position, but that was the last thing she needed. "Jacqueline's dinner will be over at nine. I'll be back before then."

Ben gave her a brief nod, which she took as a dismissal. Given the circumstances, their conversation had gone much better than expected. Even so, Terri would have felt far more comfortable about it if he'd screamed at her.

Chapter 12

Not surprisingly, Chris and Joey didn't seem the slightest bit disappointed that Ben had declined their dinner invitation. Driving a beat-up old Jeep, they took Terri to a cozy little Italian place in Murrell's Inlet that had a view of the bay and comfortable paneled booths, but there was one little problem she discovered as she scanned the menu.

"No jalapeño poppers."

"We didn't think you'd be happy if we just went to Arby's," Chris said. "This place is a little fancier, and you deserve the best. Besides, I'd just as soon you didn't eat too many hot peppers."

The implication was clear. "And by that, I suppose I need to save room for dessert?"

Joey grinned. "Yeah, you're having Chris and Joey Popsicles."

Terri glanced at her watch. "I told Ben I'd be home before nine."

Joey gasped in dismay. "You mean you can't spend the night with us?"

"No, I can't." Terri gave him an apologetic smile. "Look, the only reason I'm here is because my boss doesn't want to be left alone with Ben—especially at night."

"Well, then no wonder he's got the hots for you!" Joey exclaimed. "He's not getting any."

"Hasn't for a while, either. Their relationship is…" Terri paused, trying to think of a description that would apply in this case, but failed.

"Nonexistent?" Chris suggested.

"Just about," she agreed. "I still don't believe he likes me the way you think he does, though. I drive a lot of people crazy and Ben is one of them. Even my mother thinks I'm strange."

Joey frowned. "Why, what's wrong with you? You don't drive me crazy."

"It has to do with the way I talk—or rather the way I *don't* talk," she replied. "Most of the time I don't say much and it bothers some people."

"You talk to us," he countered.

"I know." She shook her head in disbelief. "The odd thing is that I've only known you two since yesterday. Maybe it's the sex that makes me so chatty."

Chris chuckled. "So, dear old Dad just has to nail you to get you to talk to him, huh?"

Terri rolled her eyes. "Maybe, but I don't think he wants to. He slept in the same room with me last night, and I didn't even know he was there until I woke up this morning. He does like to talk, though. You should have heard him in the grocery. He must've asked me a hundred questions, although he doesn't seem to want to talk to me at all now. I think he's miffed because I left him for you guys." Actually, he'd seemed sort of unhappy the night before and also at breakfast, which might have been Jacqueline's fault.

"Well, we *are* more fun," Joey said smugly. "I mean a guy who won't even do anything when you're sleeping in the same room with him is—"

"Married. Whether they're happy together or not, they *are* still husband and wife, and I don't want to end up in a worse predicament than I'm in already—and I certainly don't want to end up getting fired because of it."

"I see your point," he said. "I fucked my boss's daughter once and got myself canned. Of course, he didn't know I'd done his wife, too."

Terri shook her head in wonder. "You guys have no conscience whatsoever, do you?"

"Nope," Joey replied. "Not when it comes to sex. We really like it."

"Think you'll ever get married?"

"Maybe," he said with a shrug. "If I can find a girl who wants it all the time like I do."

Considering the way these two could make a woman feel, that didn't sound very difficult, although she doubted that either of them considered their "Vacation Ladies" as worthy candidates for matrimony. Terri thought it would be weird being married to a woman who'd been in a threesome with you and your best friend—though Chris and Joey might've had a different opinion.

"Most of my girlfriends get tired of it after a while," Joey went on. "I have a tendency to wear them out."

"Yeah, mine don't get much sleep, either," Chris agreed. "I guess that's why we go through them so fast."

Which made their girlfriends sound a bit like running shoes. Perhaps they were. Wear them for a while and then grab a new pair. "Ever fall in love?"

"Oh, all the time," Joey said. "It just doesn't ever last very long."

From Terri's current standpoint, it was clear that neither of them had ever taken an arrow in the chest. It might take a while—Terri was older than either of them—but it would happen someday. She only wished she could be there to see "the look" when it finally happened.

Priceless...

For now, Terri only wanted to figure out a way to spend the night with them without having to be devious about it. She knew Jacqueline would stay well away from Ben; she just wasn't sure it would work both ways. Waiting until they were both asleep was an option, but there was that sneaking thing again. Terri wasn't a child and they certainly weren't her parents.

No, they were simply the strangest damn people she'd ever met. She was beginning to wonder if her job was even worth all the hassle. With two sweet, adorable guys to cater to her every whim for a few days, not surprisingly, she was looking forward to enjoying every minute of it—*without* having to worry about Ben and Jacqueline.

After a terrific dinner, they went to Broadway at the Beach. Terri bought a black T-shirt at *Tiki Jim's* that said to *Take life with a grain of salt, a slice of lime, and a shot of tequila...* and she changed into it before they went to one of the clubs. Once there, Terri danced with her two sweet, adorable guys. Both of them. Together. At the same time.

She drew a few envious glares from some of the other girls, which was heady stuff for a woman who'd never dated anyone before. With all the excitement, keeping track of the time was the last thing on her mind, especially after they'd bought her a few drinks.

When they finally went back to the Jeep and drove off with Chris at the wheel and Joey and her in the back seat, she might've had no clue where they were headed, but something told her she was about to discover the joy of oral sex. Her suspicions were confirmed when Joey gave her a wicked grin. Unzipping his jeans, he offered her a taste of that thick cock.

"Don't worry. It's clean. I washed it again while you were napping."

It was clean all right, and so hard, slick, and wet that it gleamed in the moonlight. Terri leaned down and gave the head a tentative lick. Salty, slippery, and warm, she sucked into her mouth—just a little at first, and then as much as she could hold. He smelled good, tasted good, and felt good, and Terri could have kept going for days on end. In fact, with regular access to a hot, hard cock, she doubted she would ever have another food craving again as long as she lived. The only down side was that they were a little cramped in the back seat and she had to let go a couple of times because she was afraid she would hurt him when they hit a bumpy place in the road.

Joey combed his fingers through her hair. "Do you like it?"

Though she was enjoying it enormously, she figured he

probably wouldn't if she happened to get a tooth into him. She let go of him and sat up. "Yes, but I think I'd rather do this somewhere more comfortable—and less bumpy. Could we go back to the hotel?"

"Sure. Hey, Chris!" Joey sang out. "Madam would like to go back to the hotel now."

Chris glanced in the mirror. "What's the matter? Doesn't she like it?" He sounded worried, which wasn't too surprising. If Terri didn't like sucking Joey's dick, Chris's probably wouldn't get any attention at all.

"I like it fine," Terri replied. "Just not in a moving vehicle. I want to get back in that nice, big bed and lie down and eat you guys up. I didn't get my poppers, so I think I should get to choose where I have my dessert."

"No problem," Chris said over his shoulder. "I'd like to watch you suck him anyway. That cock of his is a real mouthful, isn't it?"

"Yes," she agreed. "Very tasty!"

Joey leaned in for a kiss. "So are you."

He was *such* a fabulous kisser. Chris was good, but Joey made her melt. Coating her fingers with the slippery fluid oozing from the head of his cock, she slid her hand up and down his thick shaft.

"Keep that up and I'll come in your hand, baby."

"Is that a problem?"

"No, but I really wanted to come in your mouth."

Terri let go of him and moved away. "Then you'd better keep it out of my reach, because I can't resist touching it."

Joey gave her a hug and murmured in her ear. "You really like all this sexy stuff, don't you?"

"Yes, I do." Threading her fingers through his hair, she pulled him closer for another kiss. "You are so adorable...so sweet." His hair was thick and curly.

Like Ben's.

The thought struck her suddenly—unbidden and damned inopportune.

What would it be like to kiss Ben? Would it be as intoxicating? Would his arms feel as warm and strong? Would he taste the same? Would the urge to sit on his lap and slide the thick length of him inside her be as strong? Terri might have only done it once, but now that she'd had a taste of it, she knew that once would never be enough. For the first time since she'd met Constance, Terri truly understood why she chased men so relentlessly. They were addicting. Terri had pretty much decided she wanted one of her own, and it tore her heart in two to think that she might have to settle for one she didn't love. Joey was in her arms, and he could make her want him. But Ben? She'd wanted him just on the basis of a look and a smile. There was a difference.

With what Terri knew now, she could go back to her room, sleep in her bed, and sometime in the night, she could go to Ben, seeking his kiss, his caress. She'd never wanted anything quite as much and knew that from then on, whatever she did with Chris and Joey, she would imagine doing with Ben. People would be more annoyed with her than ever because her mind would *always* be somewhere else. If anything, she would end up saying less, not more.

How could she bear the thought of never touching a man again as long as she lived? She loved the feel of Joey's body pressed against hers. She couldn't help reaching for him again, knowing that she had to get all of this she could before it ended. She would probably wear *them* out in the next few days, for she had a lifetime of loving to cram into one short week. This *might* be her only chance. She would take advantage of every moment.

But something was missing. "Can I say I love you?" she asked suddenly. "I think I need to."

"You can say anything you want," Joey replied. "Whether you mean it or not. Do you want me to say it to you?"

"Doesn't matter," she whispered. "I love you." *Ben.* She didn't say the name aloud, but it was hanging there, just out of hearing. *I love you, Ben.* Terri had never said those words before—and might never say them again—but she needed to say them at least once. Still, it was Joey who took her kisses and gave her his own. Joey's warm hands on her skin and his thick, hard cock in her hand, making her wet and slick with desire. Not Ben. Never *him.*

She felt as though another arrow had pierced her heart and hoped that Joey wouldn't notice her tears. They would be too hard to explain.

Never needing anyone to hold before, Terri felt fortunate to have Chris and Joey. Granted, they were virtual strangers whom she would probably never see again, but at least they were there to discuss this whole sordid affair with her. For that was how she saw it; sordid, bizarre, and incomprehensible. She wanted it all to end, but at the same time, prayed that it wouldn't.

She tore her lips away from Joey's. "Pull over, Chris," she shouted, and as he did, she realized she didn't care where they were or who might have seen them. All she cared about was putting Ben out of her mind, if only for a moment or two. Pushing Joey onto his back, she went down on him, hard. He wanted to be sucked, so, by God, she sucked him. She held his balls in a hand wet with his own syrupy fluid and devoured him. Chris hung over the seat watching while Joey groaned in ecstasy.

"When he comes, would you back off and let it hit you in the face?" Chris begged. "I love that."

Joey had asked to come in her mouth. Obviously, she couldn't please everyone, so she decided to please herself.

All the talk must've gotten to him because Joey didn't last long. "Oh, fuck!" He gasped breathlessly as his hips lurched forward. Terri felt the first burst of fluid on the back of her tongue and pulled away to take a direct hit on the cheek. Then she went down on him again, sucking the semen out of his penis as though it would sate every hunger she'd ever had—or ever would have—as long as she lived.

His semen was mildly sweet but with a sharp tang on her tongue, and she sucked hard on him as she withdrew, scraping off every drop of it with her lips and tongue before releasing him slowly. When she went back for more, he jerked slightly, and she missed, gasping with delight as the head of his penis slid across the splash of cum on her cheek. Taking his shaft in her hand to hold it steady, she rubbed it in the semen again, thinking that she'd never felt such an intoxicating caress before. On her lips, her cheek… *"Oh…"* She closed her eyes and kept on, unable to stop.

Terri heard another groan, but it hadn't come from Joey, it came from Chris. "I've never seen *anything* like that in my life. My turn. Hurry, *please.* I'm dying here."

He certainly sounded like a dying man. Terri came out of her erotic stupor long enough to look up at him. With eyes wide open, Chris held his breath as though someone had just stabbed him in the back. It only took a moment for Terri to realize she could get more of that delectable stuff out of him. She left Joey and climbed into the front seat.

"Please," he whispered, laying back and exposing his engorged penis. "It hurts. Help…"

Not as thick as Joey's, Terri could slide his cock farther inside her mouth, although swallowing it was out of the question. Slick, salty syrup poured from the head, and he tasted so good, she suspected there was some chemical in that fluid designed to drive women insane—an aphrodisiac even more effective than alcohol in dampening inhibitions.

And to think, there are women who won't do this. They must be out of their ever-lovin' minds…

The tone of the entire evening had changed. At the hotel, Chris and Joey had been methodical and coordinated, almost business-like. They knew what they wanted and how to go about getting it. But out here in the dark beneath the moon, they seemed to have lost control. Terri was in control now—and she *liked* it.

Instead of taking Chris to the quick completion he probably wanted, Terri slowed down, teasing and licking him lightly while his cock quivered with need.

Joey hung over the back of the seat, resting his chin on one hand while stroking her hair with the other. "Try licking his balls."

Chris moaned, writhing beneath her as Terri backed up and lowered her head. She ran her tongue over him gently, feeling the skin, which had seemed rough at first, turn to silk when moistened with saliva. Joey's suggestion had apparently been a good one; Chris sucked in a ragged breath, gripping the steering wheel with one hand and the back of the seat with the other. The viscous fluid oozing from his cock ran down his shaft to puddle in his groin, and with each breath, his stomach ballooned out, becoming rigid just before he exhaled with a loud grunt. Terri was no expert, but even she could tell that this was driving him completely nuts.

Nuts... They were too big to fit both of them in her mouth at once—at least, not without hurting him—so she chose one at random and went for it. Chris responded with a strangled, inarticulate sound and his cock pulsed, sending more of the syrupy fluid gushing from his slit. Even Joey let out a groan.

Scooping up the fluid from his skin, Terri caressed Chris's cock with her slick fingers while she sucked his balls. Her own body was screaming for release, so she did her best to put him out of his misery, alternately kissing and licking him to a climax that shot out an arc of semen that hit Terri in the face and ran down her neck. She went totally wild after that, enjoying him every bit as much as she had Joey, gliding his cum-slick cock and balls over her face until she reached an orgasmic level with spasms that simply wouldn't quit.

The sexual haze that clouded her mind eventually cleared, and her memories came rushing back. *Jacqueline and Ben.* Although she had hated to break up the party, she knew it was time to go. Chris and Joey drove her back to the hotel as quickly as possible, but Terri had an idea it was already too late.

ଥରେ

Jacqueline had returned from her dinner, all right, and Ben was with her. Terri could hear the tension in their voices when she walked through the door.

Closing it firmly enough to announce her return, Terri dropped her purse and her boring old shirt off in her room before strolling casually out to the kitchen. "Sorry I'm late. I lost track of the time."

"Well, you certainly must've been having fun," Jacqueline remarked. "I've never known you to be late for anything. Love your T-shirt, by the way."

Terri acknowledged the compliment with a shrug. "How was the conference?"

"Exhausting!" Jacqueline replied, seizing the opportunity to saunter off down the hallway. "I'm heading straight to bed," she said over her shoulder. "You and *Benny* have a nice evening."

Terri stared after her retreating figure, wondering what the devil had gotten into her. *Benny?* Since when did she call him Benny? She'd placed a rather heavy emphasis on it too. What the hell did *that* mean? He always referred to her as Jackie, but—

"You might want to change your shirt, *Monica,*" Ben said, cutting into her thoughts with biting sarcasm. In response to her blank stare, he added, "Those white stains really stand out on a brand-new black T-shirt, don't they?"

Chapter 13

Terri might have been a little slow on the uptake, but the white stains reference made it pretty clear that Chris's semen had not only run down her neck, but onto her shirt, as well. She wondered if Jacqueline had noticed it. Of course, it could have been toothpaste…

Ben, however, knew precisely where Terri had been and with whom—although given where they'd had dinner, it could just as easily have been Alfredo sauce. She took a moment to decide how to respond. She could lie and say it was something else, pretend she didn't know what it was, or admit to the whole damn thing. Finally, she decided that she'd told enough lies already and was getting tired of it. Honesty *was* the best policy, after all.

She wasn't going to let Ben browbeat her over this—he had no right to govern her behavior—and she looked him right straight in the eye. "Yes, and that Chris could probably hit a target from ten feet away!" she said with genuine admiration. "I was closer than that, of course, but, I mean, *wow."*

Terri was no medical expert, but she was pretty sure Ben was in danger of having a stroke. "Careful, *Benny*," she said, matching his own sarcastic tone from a minute before. "Remember your blood pressure!"

Terri had never had the dubious honor of witnessing a man actually snarling at her before, but she suspected that if she'd been standing any closer, at the very least she would have lost an arm. She considered backing down, but she was tired of being picked on. *Who does he think he is, anyway?* Terri might have fallen for him on sight, but he didn't know that, and she shouldn't have had to answer to him for anything.

When he spoke again, it was in a hoarse, angry whisper. "Fuck you." He turned and walked away without another word.

If he only could, she thought, staring after him wistfully. After a moment's reflection she decided that he was probably as long as Chris and as thick as Joey—fucking perfect, in fact. Never having seen very many penises in her life, she had now come to the realization that there was nothing more wonderful than being up close and personal with a hard, dripping cock. Then it occurred to her that she would probably never get the chance to see what Ben carried around in his boxers. *What a shame...*

Terri glanced at her watch. It was only ten twenty, and Ben had taken a nap that afternoon. Maybe he would just watch TV in the bedroom until he got sleepy. Either way, she figured it was best to let him cool off for a while. The odd thing was, she wasn't the slightest bit angry. All she felt was regret. Regret because she knew she could do things to him that Jacqueline had never even dreamed of, could make him cry out in ecstasy, and let him fill her body with his hot, creamy semen. Terri would gladly have those children he wanted so badly and do her best to make them all as happy and healthy and well-adjusted as possible, which was about the best anyone could do for a child in this world. She could make Ben forget that Jacqueline ever existed.

Too bad she would never have the chance.

Terri pulled a Sprite out of the fridge and sat down at her laptop. After checking on a few things at the office, she took a look at her email and found one from Jacqueline.

Terri,

Thank God! I think Ben is about to give up and go home. And even if he does, you're welcome to stay on here for the entire week. After all, I owe you one! Thanks for keeping him under control. There have been a few close calls, but he usually shuts right up whenever you're around. Thanks for being so understanding about the sleeping arrangements, too. I never could stand to share a room

*with anyone, and he knows that! I don't know why he acted so put
out about it this time. I guess he didn't like the idea of sharing a
room with you, although I can't imagine why. Maybe he thought you
would think he was a creep or something because I won't sleep with
him. He hasn't bothered you, has he? I doubt if he will; he's pretty
straightlaced about such things. Anyway, keep up the good work! JT*

Straightlaced? Apparently making mousy little secretaries wear
purple bikinis didn't count. Of course, he'd never bothered Terri, at
least not in the way Jacqueline meant. She wondered again if he'd
ever cheated and didn't see how he could keep from it. Before Terri
had been with Chris and Joey, she might have assumed that it was
possible to remain faithful to a wife who didn't welcome your
attentions. She wasn't so sure about that now. Everyone had their
limits.

Terri surfed the net for a while, snacked on some Cheez-Its,
watched a couple of episodes of *Star Trek* and *Stargate SG1*—
wishing for the umpteenth time that *Farscape* had never been
canceled—and then decided to go to bed, praying that Ben was
already asleep.

She crept into the room, thinking that it at least in this case, it
would have been helpful to hear him snoring because then she could
have been sure. If he was going to fuss at her from the other bed
while she was trying to sleep, snoring was preferable, and there was
always the sofa bed if he got too annoying. Besides, who needed
sleep while on vacation, anyway? Chris and Joey wouldn't care if
she *never* got out of bed, and she could take short naps whenever she
got tired. Sneaking out to spend the night with them was an option,
but if she were to leave, Ben might bother Jacqueline.

With all the inner turmoil, falling asleep was impossible. Ben
seemed quiet enough, but she fidgeted so much she was sure she
would wake him up eventually. Of course, it would serve him right
for being so nasty. *Monica, indeed!* It wasn't as though Terri had
ever made a habit of giving blow jobs. For that matter, she'd never

done *anything* before today—which Ben couldn't possibly have known. She had never broadcast the details of her love life—or lack thereof—to the four corners of the earth, and Chris and Joey were the only ones who knew it for a fact.

Terri flipped over for about the five-hundredth time and let out a groan of misery. After such an eventful day, all she really wanted was sleep. When she'd slept in the same room with Ben the night before, there were things she hadn't fully understood. She'd had great fun with the guys today and would love to do the same things with Ben—even if he *had* pissed her off. *And even though he's married to my boss.*

Unfortunately, she still liked him, still wanted him, and probably still loved him. *That's impossible. No one can fall in love that fast.* She tried to tell herself that he probably wasn't as good as Chris and Joey—not as patient or as skilled—and he might not taste or smell right. Or his dick would be too big or too small. Terri would never know.

But she wanted to. She wanted to know every freckle, every lump or bump or smooth stretch of skin on his body. She wanted to lick his damn balls and watch his cock drip all over the place. She wanted to make him insane with desire for her and her alone. It was wrong, and she knew it, but she wanted him just the same.

Lots of married people had affairs. It happened every day. That didn't make it right, of course, but *still*... Jacqueline had said he was straightlaced. Did that mean he would never stoop to having an affair? Ever? How would he feel about having one with her? Terri had hashed this over many times before, and although she'd discounted the possibility, Chris had seemed so sure—Joey, too. *He wants you bad,* Joey had said.

They were men. They should know. Terri didn't know anything except that she'd been thinking about Ben while she was with them—or trying not to. She'd gotten into the cock-sucking thing pretty well and couldn't recall thinking about him then. Maybe that was all she had to do to get him out of her mind; suck every dick she could find and never stop. She would have to line them up. Perhaps Ben would get in that line, but after having done so many of them, she might not even notice whose cock she was sucking.

Terri glanced at the clock. *Two forty.* With an inward growl, she decided that this must be what happens when a man snarls at you right before bedtime. A man you *like,* that is. Married couples should never go to bed mad. She'd heard that somewhere. She and Ben weren't married, but they *were* staying in the same room and she'd spent an entire day with him. He hadn't spent that much time with Jacqueline in forever, and she'd never spent that much time with a man. Unfortunately, while this might have explained her reaction, it certainly didn't make it go away.

She turned over again and exhaled in disgust. Sleep simply wasn't happening, and once again, she thought about going to see Chris and Joey.

But what if they weren't exclusive? What if they had a back-up woman in case Terri had fallen through? Would she be there with them? Terri would feel pretty damn stupid if she interrupted something. Of course, there *were* two of them. Terri could have one, and that woman could have the other. Which one would Terri choose? What if they both wanted the same one? Terri finally decided that she could be happy with either of them. Maybe they could flip a coin; heads for Joey and tails for Chris. *Ha, ha, ha...*

Terri took another deep breath and blew it out slowly. Perhaps some nice, fresh sea air would help. She could go out on the balcony and maybe have the shot of tequila her T-shirt touted. She wondered how far she would have to walk to get it. Was there beer in the fridge? She honestly couldn't remember.

She was just about to throw back the covers and head for the kitchen when Ben whispered, "Can't sleep?" At least, Terri thought it was him, although she might have been hallucinating due to lack of sleep.

"No," she replied. "I can't sleep. Imagine that."

The mattress squeaked as he turned over to face her. She could just make out his form in the dim light. "Hey, look, I'm sorry I got on your case earlier. Jackie and I had… words, and then you waltz in with…well, you know. I shouldn't have said anything about that spot on your shirt. It's none of my business what you do, it's just that…" He broke off with a sigh.

Terri's evil genie was back, telling her in no uncertain terms that this was something she needed to know. "Just that, *what?*"

"Just—oh, never mind. Forget it."

"No, come on," she cajoled. "Tell me what you were going to say. You've already said plenty of mean things to me, so one more couldn't hurt. Just go ahead and get it off your chest, and then maybe at least *you* can get some sleep, even if I can't."

"You're sure about that?"

"Absolutely," she replied. "Tell me. I can't sleep anyway."

"Okay. I would have liked that spot on your shirt a whole lot better if I'd been the one to put it there."

Of all the things Terri imagined he would say at such a moment, this was not among them. Apparently Chris and Joey were right. He *did* want her. She ought to give them a call and tell them so they would sleep better. Ben would sleep, they would sleep, and Terri would never sleep again for the rest of her life. By this time, she was already feeling slightly crazed. How bad would she feel after a few years? How long could a person go without sleep before they up and died from exhaustion? *Not long. Probably less than a week.* Then again, if she was going to die anyway, she might as well tell him.

"Me too."

Having said that, she thought she might be able to sleep after all. It was certainly quiet. In fact, the silence was so complete, she didn't even think Ben was breathing. Maybe he hadn't slept in ages, either, and this was his last day. Why else would he be so quiet? He hadn't been that quiet before. Maybe he was dead.

Jacqueline looked fabulous in black and would make one helluva widow. Terri would end up in prison because she'd been the one to kill him—somehow. She wasn't sure if they could pin it on her or not. On the other hand, Jacqueline could have poisoned Ben earlier that evening, intending to make Terri her scapegoat.

Scapegoat. What an odd word. Terri paused to contemplate its origin. So many expressions had meanings that had been lost in the sands of time…

She heard Ben turn over in his bed. Having said his piece, he would sleep like a baby. He'd—

Her thoughts broke off there as her blankets were stripped from her only to be replaced by Ben. *No, I'm dreaming. I dreamed the whole thing. He's asleep and so am I. I'll wake up in the morning and none of this will have happened.*

But in Terri's dreams Ben was kissing her, spearing his fingers through her hair, devouring her lips, his tongue delving deeply into her mouth. Was he a better kisser than Joey? *Hmm…if this is my dream, then he would be, wouldn't he?*

But he wasn't. Joey would *still* have to go down as the best kisser. Ben was okay, but he was a little rough. Joey's lips had been soft, sensuous, and delicious. Ben didn't taste as good as Joey, either. It had been too long since he'd brushed his teeth and gone to bed. *This is such a crappy dream.* Terri thought she should have been able to do better than that. She loved him and wanted him, so in her dreams, he should kiss better and taste like chocolate. Or jalapeño poppers at the very least.

She never *had* gotten her poppers. Those boys owed her a large order of them. They'd promised her poppers and all she got was peanut butter and jelly, jalapeño potato chips, and a gourmet Italian dinner.

Then her dream improved as Ben crawled up over her and slid his penis past her parted lips. At least, she thought he did. Yes, it had to be. It was much too big to be anything else, and it tasted just right—hard and hot and dripping with his own brand of slick syrup. *Perfect.* As long as Chris and as almost as thick as Joey. Not too big, not too small. *Just right.*

Terri cupped his balls in her hands. They were warm and heavy. *Nice.* She let go of his cock and licked them. Ben made a sound that was a bit like a stifled sneeze but he didn't tell her to stop. Terri's only complaint was the position. She would have liked it better if he was on his back.

"Lay down."

Ben rolled over and sprawled on the bed beside her, and she crawled down between his legs and licked him. On his cock, his balls, and underneath his balls. He seemed to like that last one because he made another of those sneezing sounds. Terri wondered what he would sound like if he hadn't been trying to be quiet. After all, his wife was asleep in the next room and waking her up would have been a very bad idea. Terri didn't care; she had a luscious cock to suck. The fact that it was *Ben's* luscious cock made it that much better. She licked his balls gently and then tried sucking them both into her mouth. *A perfect fit.* Ben was holding his breath again. Terri remembered Chris telling her to keep breathing, but she was in no position to tell Ben that. He would figure it out. Surely someone had done this to him before. He'd simply forgotten.

Holding his penis in her hand, she let the fluid cover her palm and then circled it with her fingers to glide up and down his shaft. She felt his balls move inside her mouth, sliding in and out. For a moment, she didn't understand why, but then realized that he was doing it; thrusting with his hips to fuck her mouth with his nuts. She let him do it for a while and then let go of him to rub his dick on her face, slathering his syrup all over her, rubbing her nose in it, her lips, her cheeks, and then back into her mouth. There was just enough light shining in through the gaps in the curtains to see him. *Beautiful.* The most beautiful thing Terri had ever seen. Ben was lying in her bed, and she was sucking him. It was a dream, wasn't it? A dream— nothing more...

Her dream would be short. She would up wake and it would end, and then, in that infuriating way that most dreams have, it would fade. In desperation, she would chase after it, never quite reaching it until it vanished from her memory.

He pulled her up and kissed her again. Then she was beneath him, his weight on top of her, his knees nudging her legs apart, his penis poised at the apex of her thighs—pushing, shoving, demanding entry.

She let him in.

His breath caught in his throat like a sob. He was sweating so profusely, it dripped onto her face. She heard it again. No, he was crying, not sweating. Those were tears. Terri reached up and touched his cheeks to be sure. He leaned into her hand and kissed it.

Reaching around, he held her closer, burying his face in her neck as she grasped his shoulders and kissed him. He pushed deep inside her, finding places that felt so good she wanted to cry. Somewhere in the back of her mind, she knew there was a man in her arms while she dreamed that Ben was making love to her. It was probably Chris or Joey. But he felt different, smelled different, and, to be quite honest, he fucked differently. Urgent, caressing—as though he loved her, but needed her as well. Needed her for what her body could give him. A release he hadn't had in more than a year...

Surely he hadn't been completely celibate. He'd only said it was Jacqueline he hadn't been with, and he would at least be able to do it to himself. Perhaps it wasn't the same. Maybe this was better— it was certainly better for her.

He filled her, completed her, and took her beyond reason. Everything was different because she loved him. It still seemed incredible, but she knew it was true. She wanted him, needed him, and loved him, even though she barely knew him.

But she *did* know him. His name was Ben and he wanted a wife, children, and a home filled with love. He was married to Jacqueline, but it would happen, somehow. For now, he was Terri's to hold, and she wasn't about to let him go.

His rhythm slowed to a steady thud. Terri listened to the sound of him moving within her as she held him.

Oh, not yet. Don't finish yet. Kiss me again. Tell me you love me. Don't stop.

He didn't reply because she hadn't said it aloud. She only thought it, just like she always did.

Don't stop. Oh, please don't stop. Tell me you love me.

Joey would have said it. He might not have meant it, but he would have said it.

I told him I loved Ben, didn't I? I love you, Ben. I said that. I distinctly remember saying it. Oh, that feels good. So good. Talk to me. You've always been chatty before. Say something, please. I can't talk. Why can't I talk?

Ben slowed down even further and rammed her hard, stretching her to the limit. His body stiffened and he let out a sob as he reached his climax, flooding her body with his seed.

A cry escaped Terri's throat as she fell into a warm, quiet place where little sparkly things drifted past her within a dark void.

The Death Star.

It had blown up again, only this time she was on it when it exploded, not merely watching, as before. Sighing as her consciousness deserted her, she went down with the ship and into oblivion.

Chapter 14

Terri woke at eight fifteen to the sound of a knock at the door. With one swift, out-of-focus glance around the room, she took in the fact that Ben's bed was empty and his suitcase was gone, along with every other trace of him. He might never have been there at all. Jacqueline had said he was almost fed up enough to go home, and sometime during the night, he must've done just that.

Jacqueline would be overjoyed, whereas Terri was devastated. Had she only dreamed that Ben had made love with her? She'd been feeling a bit off balance and wished she'd had the excuse of being drunk, but she'd been perfectly sober. Stumbling blindly to the door, she opened it. Chris and Joey were waiting for her with hugs and kisses and plans for the day. They wanted to take her parasailing.

"You'll love it!" Joey promised her. He was in the process of telling her how much fun it was to fly over the water when Chris— good old soon-to-be-an-anthropologist Chris—noticed her mood.

"Something happened," he said flatly. "Where's dear old Dad this morning?"

"Don't know," Terri said with a shrug. "Gone."

His eyes narrowed. "As in left town?"

She nodded. "I guess so. Either that or he's gotten another room somewhere." Terri doubted that. He was probably on his way back to New York even as they spoke. She wondered if she would ever see him again.

Chris cocked his head to one side, scrutinizing her carefully. "You don't seem very happy about that."

"Not really." Which was the perhaps the biggest understatement of her understated life.

"What happened? Did he and the boss have a fight?"

Terri heaved a sigh. "Yeah. A big one, apparently."

"And?"

"Then he picked a fight with me."

"Over what?"

Terri felt a little sick at the memory. "He called me Monica."

"Monica?" Obviously he didn't get the reference. *Probably too young to remember that.*

"Yeah, Clinton's aide or assistant or whatever she was. You know, the one with the white stains on her dress?"

"Oh, yeah," he said. *"Her."*

"Yeah, *her.*"

"And what did you say to that?"

She bit her lip, remembering her taunt. *The one time I should've kept my mouth shut...* "The wrong thing, apparently."

"Did he say anything to you, or did he just leave?"

"He just said 'Fuck you' and then later on, he did. *Then* he left."

Chris seemed quite surprised at this. "He fucked you? Really? I didn't think he had it in him. I'm duly impressed. Maybe he isn't such a bad dude after all."

Joey's eyes widened and his jaw dropped. "Wow! When you lose your virginity, you really lose it! Three men in the first day? That has to be some kind of record."

"Oh, gee, thanks." Terri blew out a disgusted breath. "That makes me feel *so* much better."

Joey didn't miss a beat. "That's why we're here. C'mon, get dressed and we'll take you out for breakfast and then we'll go parasailing. You'll forget all about him."

In the face of such shining optimism, Terri could only manage a rather sickly smile. Then she remembered all the food she and Ben had brought home from the grocery. She and Jacqueline would never eat it all.

"How about we just eat here?" she suggested. "It would save some time." And money, and God knows what else. She wouldn't have to get dressed, either. She could fry bacon in her nightie. She drew the line at doing it in the nude, however, which was Joey's suggestion. They were nothing if not consistent. "You two get naked," she told them, "and I'll give you breakfast in bed."

"With dessert?" Chris asked eagerly.

Sex didn't sound quite as good this morning, but she figured she might as well enjoy them for as long as she could. It was a safe bet she'd seen the last of Big Bad Ben. "Sure."

Opting to remove his pants, but not his shirt, Chris fried the bacon while Terri scrambled the eggs and Joey made toast. He made quite a mess of it, somehow managing to get strawberry jam on his cock and balls twice before he finished the job. She was at a loss to explain how he could have dripped jam on the *under*side of his scrotum—unless, of course, he'd been standing on his head. However, since he'd asked her to lick it off each time, it was far more likely that he'd done it on purpose.

Later, while they were all lying in bed, Joey said reflectively, "You know, Chris, I don't think anyone has ever cooked for us before, have they?"

"No," Chris replied. "And I've never had breakfast with such a great view, either."

Since he was lying on his stomach between Terri's legs with his plate on her buns, she had to give credit where credit was due. "Thanks, Chris. I believe that's a first."

"Sure beats going to a restaurant," Joey declared, wiggling his hips.

Lying between Joey's legs with her plate on his stomach and his glistening cock nestled between her boobs, Terri tended to agree. The Coke Can was dripping like someone had given it a good shake before popping the top.

"Still want to go parasailing?" Sliding back a little, she gave the head of his cock a long lick. "Or would you rather spend the day indoors?"

"Oh, we have plenty of time," Joey assured her. "The boat

doesn't leave the dock until eleven." He flashed his killer smile and waggled his eyebrows. "We plan ahead."

"So I've noticed."

"Hey, when you're finished there," he said, taking a gander at her nearly empty plate, "I think there's a little strawberry jam left on my balls. They feel sort of sticky."

The memory of Ben's nuts in her mouth came back to haunt her. "What's the matter? Do you think they need to have jelly all over them before I'll suck them?"

He laughed. "You like 'em plain, don't you?"

"Yeah," she replied. "But with lots of syrup. They slide better that way."

Joey frowned. "Do you have any syrup?"

Terri rolled her eyes. "No, bird-brain, I mean this stuff," she said, licking the pre-cum from his cock. "You know—all natural, no artificial flavoring, no additives, no preservatives?"

Chris laid his plate aside and smacked her on the butt. "Raise up, babe, I want some pussy for dessert."

"Well, I suppose there's no accounting for taste." She got up on her knees. "Help yourself."

Chris rolled over onto his back and pulled her down to sit on his face. His warm breath on her wet pussy sent shivers racing up her spine as his tongue penetrated her sensitive folds. Thrusting deep inside, the heat alone drew a soft moan from her, but then he began teasing her with the tip of his tongue. "Oh, *my...*"

Joey waggled his dick at her. "How 'bout sucking my cock? Ooh, and then you can lick my balls some more. I loved watching you do Chris last night. That was wild."

Chris paused, adding a heartfelt, "Yes it was" before giving a loud sniff. "Well, well, well... Dear old Dad fucked you all right, and I don't believe he used a condom. Did he?"

Terri went from hot to frigid in the space of a nanosecond, and her heart dropped like a stone. "I...I'm not sure."

Chris crawled out from under her and pulled her up to face him.

"Tell me exactly what happened. All of it."

Her mind went blank and she blinked hard, trying to remember. Obviously it hadn't been a dream. "I couldn't sleep, and I woke him up with all my tossing and turning. He apologized for fussing at me and said he'd have liked the spot on my shirt a lot better if he'd been the one to put it there. I said 'me too' and then the next thing I knew he was on top of me, kissing me. Then he moved up and put it in my mouth, and I told him to lie on his back and I sucked him for a while, then he pulled me up and kissed me again and then rolled me over and...did it."

Chris groaned. "You're sure he didn't stop to put on a condom?"

Terri shook her head. "I don't remember. I...I don't think so, but—"

"Shit, shit, *shit!* You *do* realize that if you get pregnant, he'll just say it was one of us, don't you?"

"Yes, but you two are very careful," Terri insisted. "He wasn't. There are tests and...and everything."

"Yeah, well, condoms have been known to break. Besides, he's your boss's husband," Chris reminded her. "If you accuse him, at the very least, she'll fire you."

Through the tangled mess in her mind, Terri finally saw it all, and no matter what happened, she knew she was screwed. Insisting that it was Ben's baby would get her fired. Saying it was Chris or Joey's would leave her without any support because they knew it couldn't be theirs—and Terri knew it too. That left her with two other options. Quit and get another job before Jacqueline found out about it, or tell Ben and hope he might admit to being the father and chip in with a little child support.

Then she thought of another option, which would be to let everyone assume the baby was Chris or Joey's, raise the child herself, and never tell Ben or Jacqueline anything at all. Then there was that other choice, which she couldn't even bring herself to consider. The chance that Ben might divorce Jacqueline and marry

Terri was out of the question. His leaving without a word was proof positive that he wanted nothing more to do with her. He wanted children, but she couldn't simply give her baby to him because Jacqueline wouldn't want it, and the mere thought of Jacqueline having any claim on a kid of hers made Terri's blood run cold. Someone else could adopt it, but did she really want that?

There was an excellent chance that Terri wouldn't conceive, but with Cupid and her evil genie working overtime, what were the odds of that?

"Where are you in your cycle?" Chris asked.

"Actually, I'm kind of irregular, Terri replied, trying to ignore the sinking feeling dragging her down. "Seems like I should start any day now—in fact, I'm surprised that I haven't already—but I could be wrong about that."

"Well, that's something, at least," he said. "Maybe you'll get lucky."

"Boy, you two sure know how to make a guy's dick go soft," Joey complained. "There's not a damn thing we can do about it now, except worry. Let's just fuck and then go parasailing."

Terri couldn't help but laugh. "You sure know how to cut through the crap, don't you?"

"Well, yeah," he grumbled. "I was about to get my cock sucked."

Chris shook his head sadly. "One track mind. Like I said, he's not very bright."

"Maybe," Terri admitted. "But it just so happens he's right this time—and he's also got one helluva dick there. Actually, so does Ben. I'm going to miss it, I think. Oh, shit, who am I kidding? I'll miss all three of you."

She *would* miss them—the way they looked, smelled, tasted, and felt. The way they smiled and laughed and groaned when she did something to them that they enjoyed, not to mention the things they were able to do to her. She would miss it all, because she would probably never get this lucky again. "Look, let's just forget about

Ben and getting pregnant and fired and all that. The way I see it, pregnant or not, this is my first, last, and only chance to have the time of my life. So let's do it." She looked at Chris. "Want me to douche?"

"Nah," he said with a grin. "I'll just fuck it out of you."

Joey was incredulous. "You mean you aren't going to lick the cum out of her pussy? I *love* doing that! Of course, I'd rather it to be my own and a little fresher, but—"

Terri giggled. "You really are something else, you know that?"

"Yeah," he said sheepishly. "I know. But would you suck my balls anyway?"

"Sure." Terri figured she needed *something* to get her mind off everything for a while. She also knew that given time to work through the problem, her brain would come up with the perfect solution without any help from her. It always did. She wasn't the executive assistant to the boss from hell for nothing.

"And sit on my face?" he asked hopefully. "I never get the chance when we do these summer things, 'cause we always use condoms, and I love licking a pussy with cum in it. Please?"

"Are you sure?" Terri was having a hard time believing that this sort of thing would be a turn-on for anyone, and if she'd known they were coming over for breakfast, she probably would have taken a bath first.

"Oh, yeah!" Joey assured her. "Absolutely!"

"But what will Chris do?"

"I dunno…watch?"

She glanced at Chris. "Any problem with that?"

"Nope," he replied. "Watching is good. But you could put a hand on my cock if you like. That way I won't feel so left out."

"Do you guys have *any* inhibitions at all?"

They shook their heads.

These two were also rapidly expunging every one of her own inhibitions, at least with regard to sex. She could even talk to them in complete sentences. She tried a different tack. "Ever do this with each other?"

They exchanged another of their meaningful glances.

"Well, once," Chris admitted. "We were with a lady who liked that sort of thing. It was okay, but I wouldn't kill for it. We prefer girls."

"It's nice to know you draw the line somewhere," Terri said dryly. "Still, it might be interesting to watch sometime."

"We'll do it if that's what you want," Chris said. "But we'd just as soon not."

"Okay, forget it, then. I can't believe I asked you that, anyway." Terri shook her head in disbelief. "I don't know what's gotten into me."

Joey snorted a laugh. "Uh, what about three cocks in one day? I think that might change the way you look at things."

"I see your point." She aimed a thumb in Joey's direction. "You know something, Chris? He's smarter than you think."

Chris rolled his eyes. "You didn't go through high school with him."

"Be nice, now," Joey cautioned. "I did graduate, you know."

"Just barely," Chris reminded him. "If the girls hadn't helped you study, you'd never have made it."

Joey laughed. "Who says we studied?"

Terri could see it now. Joey holding a book while one girl coached him on what to study and another girl sucked his dick. Terri had truly led a sheltered life. She'd been one of the brainy girls, but she'd certainly never "tutored" any of the boys. *The things I've missed...*

But she was making up for that lack of experience now. When she climbed on top of Joey it struck her why the number sixty-nine was so significant. She'd heard the reference before, but honestly hadn't cared enough to risk ridicule by asking someone, and she'd never quite gotten around to Googling it. *Yet another mystery solved.* Chris scooted up between Joey's legs and lay ball to ball with him, draping his own legs over Joey's. Terri had to wonder what number would stand for that. *Sixty-nine to the ninth power? Sixty-nine over six?* Who knew? All Terri could say was that it put both of their stiff cocks within range of her lousy vision—and her tongue.

Unfortunately, moving farther forward to get to both of them put her out of the reach of *Joey's* tongue. He fussed about it for a bit, but not for long, because she wound up licking both sets of balls and had a hand on each dick—one long and slender, the other thick and shorter—making them forget about anything else. Having all those nuts to suck and hard, slick cocks to handle was driving her crazy, but she did it until her own body was screaming in frustration. Her brain was screaming too, and the one thought she couldn't get out of her head was that the two of them together equaled Ben.

Something had to give. She couldn't stop thinking about him— kissing her, making love with her, and not even saying goodbye. "I don't suppose you brought any condoms along, did you?"

"Well, yeah," Joey replied breathlessly. "We don't go anywhere without them."

"Then get 'em and put 'em on," she demanded in desperation. "I want you one after the other, as hard as you can." Maybe they could fuck Ben out of her mind. She certainly hoped so because she wasn't having any luck getting rid of him on her own.

Chris went first and gave it the old college try, stretching her lengthwise, but not enough sideways. Then Joey went, filling the width, but he didn't reach far enough inside. *I need Ben,* she thought wildly. *He was perfect.* And it wasn't just his penis. The whole package deal was perfect. She wanted him and he was gone forever—the one man who fit her perfectly and made her so mad she could spit, but whom she loved anyway.

She wanted to scream her frustration. She was with two wonderful, sexy men, but neither one of them was right all by himself. Chris had the intelligence and Joey had the boyish charm. Blended together and a little older, they would have been perfect because they would have been Charles Benjamin Tremaine. The man who'd snarled at her, made mad, passionate love with her, and then disappeared in the night without a word.

Hell. This was definitely it, and she didn't even have to die to get there. She could almost see Cupid sitting on the head of the bed, giggling his little wings off while Satan had a big, belly laugh at her expense, and her evil genie was buying drinks all around. Terri told them all to go fuck themselves, which they thought was even more hilarious.

Joey let out a yell and ejaculated, but the Death Star never wavered. It simply sat there, suspended in space, taunting her just as Cupid, Satan, and the genie had. She was losing her mind. She couldn't stand it any longer. She was hanging in limbo. The man who'd just finished with her moved away. She curled up into a ball, sobbing. Ben was gone, he was never coming back, and she would never see him again. *Never, never, never.*

I find your lack of faith disturbing, Darth Vader intoned.

Oh, what the hell do you know, Darth? You're just a stupid Jedi knight who's been seduced by the dark side of the Force.

"Did we hurt her?" Joey asked, seeming completely aghast that they would have done such a thing. "We *never* hurt them!"

"I don't think it was us," Chris said quietly. "I think dear old Dad broke her heart."

Chris was such a smart fellow. And to think, three days ago Terri hadn't even known she had a heart to break. She should return it. It wasn't any good. Broken beyond repair. Substandard. Flawed. Useless. The only part of her that worked was her tear ducts, and they were stuck in crying mode.

Someone took her in his arms. *Chris.* He held her close and rocked her and told her she'd be okay. He seemed so sure she wasn't dying, but Terri was hard to convince. Joey got her a drink. She had no idea what it was. *Probably cranberry juice.* Then he wiped her face with a wet washcloth. They were trying to help her, but it wasn't working. She couldn't remember crying like this. *Ever.* It was as if every tear she ought to have shed in her life was falling now. She felt lifeless, hopeless. Near death…

Terri! A disembodied voice called out to her.

"Ben?"

You will go to the Dagobah system. It was Obi Wan's ghost!

And Luke answered him, clearly mystified. *Dagobah system?*

There you will learn from Yoda, the Jedi master who instructed me.

The apparition faded. *Ben, Ben!* Luke called. But it wasn't Luke, it was Terri shouting those words.

She must have sounded damn silly. These two were trying to help her, and she was off somewhere in a galaxy far, far away hollering for Ben Kenobi. *Okay. Enough is enough. Stop crying. You can do it. Stop. Now. Han Solo is here on a Tauntaun to save you. No, wait—it's Chris and Joey. They'll help you if you'll let them.*

"Come on, Terri," said Chris. "Try to stop now. Take a deep breath. You'll be okay. Don't let him do this to you. Keep breathing." He'd told her that when he was trying to fuck her ass, and it had felt so astonishingly good. These were nice people. They would help. They would understand. Terri had no one else to turn to, except her boss. *Jacqueline?* How she would laugh if she knew the truth. "Ben?" she would say. "You're in love with Ben? Are you out of your mind?" And Terri would have to say that yes, indeed, she was—stark, raving bonkers.

"I think she's better now, Chris," Joey said. "Come on, Terri. Let's go take a shower. Just you and me, okay? It'll make you feel better."

Terri hiccupped and finally found her voice. "You're both so sweet. I'll try." She sat up and Joey wiped her face again. "I'm so sorry. I couldn't stop thinking about him. I thought if you—" Her voice cracked and she leaned her head back, exhaling sharply. "I thought you could make me forget. It made it worse, though." She felt the tears coming again and fought to keep them in check. Keep breathing, Chris had said. He was right. It did help.

Joey took her hand and helped her up, letting her lean on him. "A nice, hot shower makes everything better. C'mon, you'll see."

"What about Chris? I thought you did everything together."

"He held you while you cried," Joey replied. "Now it's my turn."

She should have known. These two planned for everything. They probably had a contingency plan for this scenario all worked out down to the last detail. Considering everything else they'd done, this strategy was bound to be effective.

Chris turned on the water while Joey held her and then helped her into the tub, standing her under the hot spray. She stood like a statue while he washed her hair and her entire body. Pulling her into his arms, he massaged her back, and then bent his head to kiss her. He might not have been quite up to rocket science, but he could kiss with the best of them.

"You'll get over it," he said. "Trust me. It happens to me all the time. I find a girl to love with all my heart and just when I think it'll last forever, I get kicked in the nuts. But the pain goes away. It just takes a while."

"Is that why you do this?" Terri asked. "So you won't get hurt?"

Cocking his head to one side, he considered this for a moment. "Maybe. I don't know. I guess it's a little safer knowing we won't be trying to stay together forever. It's that forever thing that causes all the trouble."

Terri nodded. She hadn't given it much thought before, but she was sure he was right. She wanted Ben forever. *That* was why it hurt so much when he left. "Thank you for being here," she whispered, leaning closer to kiss him on the neck. "I don't know what I would have done without you."

"You would have gotten through it somehow," he assured her. "I do it alone most of the time, but it helps to have someone."

Since she'd never had this problem before, she would have to take his word for it. She felt sorry for him. The way he talked, this sort of thing had happened to him several times. Terri didn't think she could live through it more than once and hoped she didn't make a habit of falling in love with men she couldn't have.

Chapter 15

Ben still couldn't believe what he'd done. He'd actually cheated on his wife, and with her assistant, no less. The only thing that would've made it more of a cliché would have been if Terri had been his assistant, rather than Jackie's. About all he could say for himself was that he hadn't raped her. She'd been willing. No woman could do what Terri had done without some small inkling of desire.

He sat on the plane to New York with his eyes closed, savoring those moments with Terri while mentally kicking himself for doing it at all. Jackie wasn't the only woman he'd ever made love to; there had been others prior to his marriage. He knew how good it could be. Or rather, he *thought* he knew. Terri had blasted every sexual encounter he'd ever had into oblivion—doing things to him that no one else had ever done, and doing them in a way that made each one of them feel like an act of love, not simply as a means of slaking his lust—or hers.

The worst part of it was, he didn't know one damn thing about her. Had no idea whether she was a practiced courtesan or simply an enthusiastic amateur. Jackie had never told him anything about Terri's private life; in fact, if asked, she'd probably have said that Terri didn't have one. Even if Jackie had known about Terri's experiences with the opposite sex, he couldn't very well ask his wife if her assistant was normally a slut or a nun.

If Ben had to choose, he would have said Terri was more along the lines of a nun, but without the cloistered lifestyle. The way she'd behaved in the airport and then when they arrived in Myrtle Beach didn't fit the slut description at all. She'd seemed painfully shy, although her attitude had changed when they were out on the beach.

They'd had fun together. He knew they did. But then her attitude changed again. Somewhere along the line, he'd missed something. *Something important.*

There was no question of continuing his farce of a marriage to Jackie. He would find a good lawyer as soon as he got back to New York. All he wanted was the house he'd grown up in. She could have everything else. The other assets would be divided and then, when the divorce was final, he would find Terri and try to explain. Somehow. Of course, that would be tough to do when he couldn't explain it to himself.

He could have left Jackie for any number of women over the past ten years. Gorgeous, intelligent, vivacious, sexy women. What was it about Terri that had made him crack? She was certainly intelligent, but she wasn't any of those other things. Well, she *was* sexy, but did he think it simply because she'd been sleeping in the same hotel room with him? He'd never been that close to any other woman since his marriage—not even his wife. Perhaps that was the answer.

Maybe he had something to prove to himself. He knew it was pretty shallow, but men had been motivated by less. Jackie had rebuffed him for so long he was beginning to question his appeal and Terri had been whooping it up with *two* men. Maybe one man wasn't enough for her. If he could satisfy her as well as they could, he might prove to her, as well as himself, that he was as good a lover as any other man.

Or was it jealousy? Even that was no excuse, but it might at least explain his behavior. Still, no matter how jealous he might have been, he should've had more control over his actions. After all, that ability to control impulses was what set humans apart from the animals. If he'd been an animal, he wouldn't have taken no for an answer from Jackie.

Terri hadn't said no. He'd been brutally honest with her, had told her exactly how he felt and what he wanted. And what had she said? *Me too.* He hadn't dreamed it, and nothing she'd done after that made him believe she hadn't meant it. But it was wrong. He didn't want to be a part of a sordid extramarital affair, and he didn't want Terri to be a part of that, either. She deserved better.

It was so ironic. If he'd divorced Jackie years ago, he would have been free to be with Terri, but without Jackie, he would never have met Terri.

Ben knew that leaving in the middle of the night was cowardly. He should've stayed and told Jackie what he felt and what he intended. Then he wouldn't have had to sit in the airport half the night waiting for a flight and wouldn't now be sick and exhausted on a plane bound for home. Part of what pushed him into leaving was the notion that if Terri had been with those two boys, she could probably convince any man he was different, special, heroic. For a short, ecstatic space of time, she'd certainly made Ben believe it of himself.

Ben knew he was no hero. He was a human man with human failings, and he'd done the wrong thing with Jackie so many times, it was pathetic. He'd ticked off Terri, too. However, he was also beginning to believe that, at least where Jackie was concerned, there *was* no right thing to do. Terri was a different story altogether.

If you leave your wife, leave because you want to leave, not because you want someone else.

Ben had heard that pearl of wisdom somewhere along the line and thought perhaps it had motivated his choice. He needed to tie up the loose ends and then dedicate himself to finding out if there was any true feeling for him behind Terri's enigmatic little face. She was such a puzzle, and he had a feeling he might never be a part of it or find the solution.

ഇരുൽ

Terri had a hard time not comparing parasailing with the day she'd spent on the beach with Ben. Both times she'd laughed and screamed as though she was having the time of her life, but playing in the sand with Ben eclipsed hanging out with Chris and Joey and flying over the ocean. So what if she'd made more of it than it really was? It was still the best day of her life, even if it *was* only a day at the beach with Ben, her boss's husband who she was there to keep occupied and hopefully irritate so much that he would go home.

Jacqueline would be duly impressed that Terri had accomplished her mission in only two days. She might even add on a nice, fat bonus to the vacation time she'd promised. A week of paid vacation to anywhere... Terri could just picture the look on Jacqueline's face when she told her she wanted to spend a week at Ben's house.

After their parasailing adventure, the guys took Terri to Arby's, and she finally got her jalapeño poppers. Sitting in a booth with her two adorable boyfriends and a large, piping hot order of poppers, a package of creamy ranch dressing, and a salt shaker should have been enough to make her life complete—and would have been if only she could exchange Chris and Joey for Ben.

"You're certainly easy to please," Chris commented. "Cheap, too. At this rate, we'll have money left over at the end of the week ."

"That's me—cheap and easy." Never having considered herself to be easy *or* cheap, she tried to laugh it off, but she wasn't very proud of herself. Now that she'd had time to think about it, she felt sort of icky—like the scummy floor of a movie theater. On top of that, she might be pregnant. What kind of mother would she make? As little as she talked, the poor kid would probably have delayed speech development. She would have to put him in daycare and speech therapy and hope for the best.

Joey slid an arm around her, pulling her close and kissing her lightly on the cheek. "No you aren't cheap and you aren't easy. What you are is the best girl we've ever had."

The last time they'd been in bed together, she'd cried her eyes out. "Oh, so crying is a good thing? I wouldn't have thought it, myself."

"It's the vulnerability factor," Chris stated firmly. "That and the bikini. Displaying your navel shows your maternal side."

Where the hell does he get this stuff? "Maternal? You mean you're looking for a mother?"

He laughed and took a sip of his Coke. "Not exactly."

Terri stared at him blankly.

"Not someone to be *our* mother, but someone to have our children. All male-female interactions are based on it. Women look for strong, healthy men who would be good providers and protectors, and who would also be able to sire healthy children. Men look for female bodies with a smaller waist to accentuate the hips and breasts, which suggest good child-bearing and nurturing capabilities." He shrugged and shook his head. "We can't help it. It's innate."

Joey gave Terri a squeeze. "He loves to spout off shit like that. Now, me, I just do whatever my dick tells me. If I look at a woman and my dick gets hard, I go after her."

Terri had to laugh. "Sounds like you're both saying exactly the same thing. You just have a different way of putting it."

"No," Chris said. "He reacts, whereas I know *why* I react, and I focus on what it is about someone that attracts me. It's very interesting."

Maybe for a lab rat. She cleared her throat. "I'll take your word for it. But be honest, now. When you first laid eyes on me, what did you think?"

Chris leaned back in his seat, his lips curled into a smile that could have stolen a much tougher heart than Terri's. "You were looking at us, which indicated that you weren't entirely satisfied with the way things were going in your life, and you made eye contact. That's very important."

That explains why men have never shown an interest in me before. On those rare occasions when she *did* look at a man, she almost never looked them in the eyes. It was sort of like getting caught with her hand in the cookie jar. "What else?"

"Well, like I said before, there was the bikini. You can't hide much from a man's eyes when you're wearing something like that."

"No shit," Joey snickered.

Chris shot him an admonitory glance before continuing. "And you know, being rail-thin may be the fashion, but most guys like a woman with a little bit of extra padding. I think that's programmed into us too, because, if you think about it, a really thin woman might be unhealthy."

Joey groaned and ran a hand through his curls. "You take all the fun out of it, Chris. I like women who aren't super thin because their tits are usually bigger. I like them big, that's all. I don't think about whether she looks healthy or not."

Chris chuckled. "You don't think about it because it's part of your programming to like big tits and wide hips."

Which describes me to T. "Okay then, explain something else. Why do men prefer blonde bimbos over the more intelligent women? I mean, wouldn't looking for a healthy, *intelligent* woman be the best thing for the survival of the species?"

Chris replied without hesitation. "It's fear."

"Of what?"

"That a woman might be smarter than you are."

"Why would that frighten you?"

"Don't know," he replied with a shrug. "It just does. Maybe it's because if a woman is smarter than you are, she'll think you're an idiot and not want you. A less intelligent woman would look up to you more."

Terri bit into another popper and nearly had a food-induced orgasm, so it took her a moment to ask another question. "But doesn't it work the other way around? I mean, why would *anyone* want to have children with someone too stupid to live? That doesn't bode well for the overall intelligence of the species as a whole. Finding a mate who is both healthy *and* intelligent would seem to me to be the best way to go, and yet, the bimbo still rules. Explain that."

"You got me," he declared, throwing up his hands. "Maybe that sort of thing is more cultural than biological."

So, Mr. Anthropologist can't explain everything. Although it might explain why Ben had climbed into her bed—it was that damned bikini. If Terri hadn't been displaying her navel like the poster model for *Moms 'R' Us*, he never would have given her a second thought. It was all *his* fault. He'd been the one to foist that purple bikini on her. True, he couldn't very well make her wear it, but he'd certainly encouraged her. She would remember his jaw-dropping reaction until her dying day.

"Hey, can we talk about something else?" Joey complained. "This is getting way too technical. It ruins it for me if I start thinking about why I like someone or why I don't."

Terri nodded. "I don't think I want to delve too deeply, either." Nor did she want Joey to get so bummed out that he stopped what he was doing. She felt warm and cozy in his arms, and his heart beating against her shoulder blade was very comforting. She didn't want to spoil the intimacy with too much analysis.

Joey nuzzled her ear. "Fortunately all this talk hasn't ruined me yet. My dick is still hard as a rock. So, how about it, Terri? Think you can forget him long enough to have some more fun with us?"

She would probably start bawling again, but she *had* gotten her poppers, and a deal was a deal. "I'll try, but I do need to talk to Jacqueline this afternoon. I don't think there's anything going on at the conference tonight, unless she's having dinner with some of her cronies. The thing is though, with Ben gone, she won't need me anymore and she'll probably send me back to New York."

"Doesn't matter," Chris said. "If you want to stay the full week, you can share a room with us. It would make everything a lot easier, and we'd love to be able to spend the night with you."

"I'll keep that in mind if she acts like she wants me out of there. Spending a vacation with my boss doesn't appeal to me very much, even if she *is* gone most of the time." She paused, shuddering at the thought of spending another day with Jacqueline. "I mean, people usually go on vacation to get *away* from their boss, not to get closer to them."

"No shit," Joey remarked. "C'mon, let's go get your stuff now.

You can just leave her a frickin' note."

Terri hesitated. "I hate to be a party pooper, but I don't think I can, um, *do* it with you guys anymore."

Chris nodded as though he understood. "Messed you up big time, didn't he?"

"Yeah." She sighed, leaning back against Joey. Whether she ever slept with him again or not, he certainly had a good shoulder to cry on. "I believe he did."

Joey planted a kiss on her cheek. "Doesn't matter. We'll have tons of fun whether we fuck or not."

"You're sure about that?"

"Absolutely. It's all about having a good time, and, like I said, you're the best girl we've ever had. I'm not saying it wouldn't be great if we could fuck you constantly, but—"

"Sex isn't everything," Chris said firmly.

Terri wasn't sure they meant it, but they hadn't lied to her yet. Still, they did have penises and therefore weren't trustworthy.

Then again, maybe Constance was wrong about that.

Chapter 16

"Terri? Is that you?"

Groaning inwardly, Terri followed the sound of Jacqueline's voice to the spacious, elegant bathroom where she was currently engaged in becoming even more stunning than usual. "Yes, it's me. I see you're going out."

"Yes, I've made an absolutely fabulous contact!" With a smile so big Terri could see the smudge of lipstick on her teeth, Jacqueline looked like a piranha about to strike. "This could turn out to be the most lucrative conference I've ever attended."

Found love, did you? Well, as it happens, so have I. Three of them, in fact—and one of them was yours. Terri would've given a lot to see the look on Jacqueline's face if she'd had the guts to say it aloud—not that this new contact could have *anything* to do with love. "That's nice."

Jacqueline peered past her. "Where's Ben? Isn't he with you?"

"He's gone."

"Gone?" Jacqueline's eyes danced with delight as she stepped out into the hallway wearing nothing but a bra and panties and a slip. Her face was only half done and her hair was wet, but she was still devastatingly beautiful. Like Marilyn Monroe, she would have looked good in a paper sack. "Really? As in back to New York?"

"I don't know." Terri shrugged, wishing she *did* know, because all she wanted was to see him again and tell him *anything* to get him to come back. For once in her life, she wouldn't hold her tongue.

Jacqueline persisted. "His suitcase is gone too? Everything?"

Terri nodded. Oh, yes, he was gone, and he had, indeed, taken everything. *Including a big, fat chunk of my heart.*

Well, maybe not *everything*. He might've left a little something else behind for her to remember him by. A small token of his affection, perhaps, the existence of which only time and a pregnancy test would reveal.

"That's wonderful!" she exclaimed. "What on earth did you do to make him leave?"

Terri shrugged again with a nonchalance she certainly didn't feel. "Don't know." *I sucked the man's cock and balls and then let him fuck the living snot out of me. It should have had the opposite effect, but what the hell do I know?*

"Ignoring him usually works for me," Jacqueline declared. "He can't stand the cold shoulder or the silent treatment. It drives him nuts when I won't talk to him! Even more so than arguing."

That explained a lot. Why Cupid had matched her up with a man who *needed* conversation was one of the more ironic twists of fate Terri could imagine. *If I ever get my hands on that damned Cupid, I'll rip his wings off. Feather by painful little feather. Then I'll break all his arrows and stomp on them.* Torturing Cupid wouldn't change anything, but it might make her feel better knowing he'd suffered as much as she had.

"Well, you're off the hook then," Jacqueline said. "As far as I'm concerned, you can either stay for the full week or go on back to New York. It doesn't matter anymore." She heaved a huge sigh of obvious relief. "I'm just glad he's gone! It's such a pain when he gets pushy. I told him long ago I didn't want to waste time having children, and he understood that—or so I imagined. We were doing fine until he got this procreation idea stuck in his head."

Having heard Ben's side of the story, Terri doubted they'd ever been "fine." Jacqueline had simply been pulling the wool over her husband's eyes. Repeatedly. The obvious solution was divorce, but if Jacqueline couldn't see it, having her assistant point it out wouldn't make the slightest bit of difference. "Then I'll leave."

Jacqueline laughed, sounding a bit like the Wicked Witch of the West. "I guess having to be here with Ben would make anyone want to go home, but I *did* promise you an extra week of vacation."

"I know. I'll be back at work on the Monday after next." Just in time to put in for a maternity leave. She would have to check with the personnel department. Maybe she wouldn't have to do it right away.

Terri went to pack up her things, wanting to get out of there as quickly as possible. This was probably how Ben had felt when he left. At least he'd had a car and could leave whenever he wanted. *Thank God for Chris and Joey.*

A few minutes later, Terri headed out with her fully packed suitcase, laptop, and purse in hand.

Jacqueline stuck her head out through the bathroom door. With only one set of lashes mascaraed, she looked quite comical—for a change—and more than a little surprised. "You're leaving right now?"

Terri nodded and opened the door to the condo. Chris and Joey promptly stepped in to take her bags.

If Jacqueline had seemed surprised before, she was completely bowled over at the sight of Terri's new friends. "Who—?"

"Chris and Joey," Terri replied. "I'll be staying with them."

Jacqueline blinked and then her eyes widened to the point she would probably need a plastic surgeon to repair the damage. "There are *two* of them?"

"Yeah," Terri said with what she hoped was a smug little smile. "They make a great team."

Chris and Joey both grinned and waved as they headed for the elevator. Jacqueline stood staring after them, her mascara wand seemingly forgotten in fingers that had apparently gone numb.

"I hope you enjoy the rest of your vacation, Jacqueline." Smiling sweetly, she aimed a meaningful glance at the guys. "I know I will."

As she turned to go, Jacqueline put a hand on her arm. "Wait a minute. You mean you…?" She wasn't able to finish her sentence, but her meaning was quite clear.

Terri gave her a casual nod. "Oh, yeah. Both of them. Together. At the same time."

As parting shots go, it was one of Terri's better ones, remarkable—unlike a great many others—for actually having been spoken aloud. Leaving the room with every intention of not looking back, she simply couldn't resist the temptation to steal a peek over her shoulder. Although she suspected it might wind up costing her in the end, it was a sight Terri would remember until her dying day.

Despite the look of dazed shock on her face, her boss from hell was still as beautiful as ever, but her mascara wand had hit the floor.

౸ఐ

For the remainder of the week, Chris and Joey kept Terri so busy she didn't have much time to think about Ben and she fell asleep in their arms, completely exhausted each night. The perfect companions, they kept their promise and didn't insist on having sex with her, even though they did share a bed. Knowing she would miss them dreadfully, she cried quite a few tears at their parting, but she also knew it was time to put Myrtle Beach behind her and head for home.

Unfortunately, Cupid had the last laugh, and a home pregnancy test only confirmed what she already knew.

She was going to have a baby.

Chapter 17

Terri's only saving grace was that Jacqueline had known she was with Chris and Joey that week and would have no reason to suspect that her husband had been the one to actually do the honors. That the baby was his was beyond doubt; Chris and Joey had been very meticulous about birth control. Ben hadn't given it a thought, and a DNA test would prove it.

The last thing Terri wanted to do was to hound Ben into paying child support or anything else. She still didn't understand why, but he was gone. He'd done his thing and left that night, leaving no note, no promises, and no goodbyes. Knowing how much he wanted a family while she had a nice little bun baking in the oven gnawed at her continuously. She should tell him—his phone number was right at her fingertips on a daily basis, which was unnecessary because she'd memorized it; home, office, and cellular—but every time she tried to call, she chickened out. He'd left her that night without a word. If he wanted her, he should have said so.

The temptation to pick up the phone gradually lessened after a few weeks as she focused on more important matters—the most pressing of which was what to do with the baby.

Adoption became less of an option every day because she was talking to the baby all the time. For some reason, she thought of it as a boy. Never having talked to men very much in her whole life, she'd gotten used to the idea while on vacation, and now, talking to women wasn't her only option. In fact, she talked to them less than ever. She didn't tell Constance about her escapades in South Carolina and doubted she ever would. At some point her pregnancy would become obvious, thus proving she was no longer a virgin, but she kept quiet, putting off requesting a family leave until the last possible moment.

Terri scheduled an appointment with her gynecologist, who was now her obstetrician. Her child would be born in April, when the dogwood trees and tulips were in bloom. She spent her spare time researching schools, daycare centers, and pediatricians with her usual efficiency, and these choices were made within a few weeks of her return. Waiting to tell Jacqueline was another choice she made. She would find out soon enough.

Interestingly enough, Jacqueline made no mention of the time they'd spent down south. If she had any questions about Terri's two boyfriends, she kept them to herself, and if she'd heard anything from Ben, she kept that to herself too.

Constance, however, couldn't keep her mouth shut about much of anything. "You look like you're gaining weight, Terri. If I didn't know better, I'd swear you were pregnant."

Since this was said within the hearing of at least ten other people, Terri chose not to reply, hoping that everyone would think Constance was picking on her weight, rather than announcing her pregnancy. No one else would care or even notice, much less make mention of the fact that she looked different, although she knew it was true. She was already up a cup size in bras, and her clothes were getting tight around the middle. She could have claimed a cupcake addiction, but, in truth, she'd been eating jalapeño poppers like they were going out of style. The folks at Arby's knew her on sight and would put a batch in the fryer the moment she walked through the door.

Her emotions were so volatile, she cried every time she ate any poppers because they reminded her of Chris and Joey—those two sweet, adorable guys whom she would never see again. She missed them terribly and regretted not having any pictures of them, let alone a phone number to call. It hurt like hell, but she couldn't seem to stop, not really caring that the people in Arby's probably thought she was nuts for eating them when they made her cry so much. She would bawl like a baby and then slip back into neutral—except, of course, when she ate a pizza covered with jalapeños, which made her cry even more because she'd shared a pizza with Ben. Since it took her a few days to recover, she could only do that once a week.

Now Constance thought she looked fat. The mean, skinny little slut! How dare she say that? Terri wanted to claw her eyes out—and that was before Constance added insult to injury by telling her she was turning into quite the butterball.

Terri regarded her with a single raised eyebrow. "So?"

"Well, you'll never get a man looking like that!" She snickered. "Not in this town!"

Nope, just in Myrtle Beach. All things considered, Terri had done pretty well there, which was a miracle in and of itself. "Don't need one."

"Oh, yeah, that's right. I forgot you don't like men, do you?"

"They're okay," Terri said with a shrug. She'd known at least three that she'd liked. She did her best to make her mind as blank as her expression, because if she'd thought about it for another moment, she would have been crying in her jalapeños again.

"You should join a club," Constance suggested. "I work out every other day. Maybe you should come with me."

Terri declined the invitation, knowing that while Constance *did* go there for her health, the gym was also where she found a lot of her boyfriends. Terri didn't want to find a boyfriend. She wanted Ben. Besides, Constance probably only wanted Terri there with her to make her look thinner and prettier and sexier and—

"Terri," Jacqueline called from her doorway. "I've got to be out of the office for an hour or two. Would you cancel my next three appointments?"

Terri gave Constance a perfunctory smile and went back to her desk. *Saved by the boss from hell...*

Sitting down heavily in her chair, Terri reached for the phone, wondering what had come up that was so damned urgent. She chuckled to herself thinking that maybe Jacqueline was also expecting and had run off to her doctor, or—what would have been more likely—to an abortion clinic. What a laugh it would have been if Ben had gotten *both* of them pregnant during that vacation.

Terri had tried to come up with a good reason for Ben's behavior and still couldn't figure it out. He must've assumed she was on some form of birth control or she wouldn't have been messing around with Chris and Joey. Still, he might have asked. Or she could have mentioned it. Or she could have just said no.

And, by the same token, hell could freeze over, taxes could become a thing of the past, and the price of gasoline could drop to five cents a gallon.

Jacqueline came out of her office in a rush. "Got those appointments canceled?"

Terri didn't even look up. "Working on it."

"Men!" she growled. "If it's not one thing, it's another! I should take you with me. It certainly worked before."

Jacqueline was already striding toward the elevator and had nearly reached it when her meaning finally sunk in. *Ben! She's going to see Ben!*

"Say hello for me," Terri called out, but she doubted that Jacqueline even heard her because she never stopped or even registered the fact that Terri had spoken to her. The doors slid closed behind her with the finality of a coffin lid.

Terri stared after her for a long moment. *There goes the luckiest woman in the whole, wide world. She has it all. And me? I'm just her assistant.* Swallowing hard, she stared at her computer. *I should quit this job right now and never come back.* The place where Cupid's arrow had struck began to ache again—she'd given up on the idea that the pain was the result of anything else. Her eyes filled with tears that splashed on her glasses as they dripped from her lashes and rolled down her cheeks. Closing her eyes, she pressed her lips together, trying desperately to stave off the sobs, but it was impossible.

It took her a minute, but she finally got herself under control and started calling to cancel Jacqueline's appointments. Once she'd finished, she simply sat there, unable to recall what else she was supposed to do. She stared at her computer until the screen saver started up, and then sat watching the bouncing ball for what seemed like days.

I've got to get out of here. A glance at the clock revealed that she'd been sitting there doing nothing for two solid hours.

The phone was blinking. Terri picked it up and simply said hello. She couldn't remember what to say, or even where she was. If anyone had noticed she'd been off in La-la Land, they hadn't bothered to comment.

"Where the hell is she?" a man's voice demanded. "She was supposed to be here an hour ago!"

Terri was dumbfounded. "Who?"

"Jackie!" he exclaimed. "We were supposed to be meeting with the lawyers. And I've been calling for the past forty minutes! Don't you ever answer the damned phone?"

"What?"

"If you're covering for her, so help me, I'll—" He broke off there. "Never mind, she's here." The phone clicked and Terri was left listening to a dial tone.

That was Ben. She'd just talked to Ben! And he'd yelled at her. *Some things never change.* "Did you hear that?" she asked the baby. "Your father was on the phone just now, and he's *still* mad at me."

A growl of protest from her stomach reminded her that she'd missed lunch. Snatching up her purse, she headed for the elevator.

She needed some poppers, and she needed them *now*.

Chapter 18

A month or so later, Terri went to personnel and filled out the forms for her leave. They might have called it a family leave, rather than maternity or pregnancy, but the effect was the same. Jacqueline was irritated.

"You can't possibly take that time off," she snapped, slamming the leave forms in Terri's inbox. "There'll be too much happening then, and I don't want to have to deal with a different assistant."

Terri stared at her blankly. This was a bit much, even for Jacqueline. *What does she think I'm going to do? Have the baby at my desk?*

Her face hardened, losing every trace of beauty. "You'll just have to tell your sister or whoever it is that you can't take time off to help out. I simply can't spare you."

Terri was rendered even more speechless than usual—until she remembered who she was talking to. *How like her not to even notice my swollen belly!* "It's for me, not my sister."

Jacqueline's jaw dropped. "Those boys in Myrtle Beach? I can't believe it! Of all the stupid, asinine things to have done—"

Somehow, Terri just couldn't let Jacqueline think that about Chris and Joey. It gave her the perfect explanation for her condition, but... "It wasn't them," she said quietly. "It was...someone else."

"Some stranger?"

Terri sighed. Trust Jacqueline to jump to a ridiculous conclusion when the truth was perfectly obvious, particularly when she knew that Terri had spent the night in the same room with Ben. *Twice.*

Lifting her chin, Jacqueline peered down her aristocratic nose at her pregnant assistant. "You should have gotten an abortion. It's what I would have done."

Terri looked her straight in the eyes. "It's not the baby's fault."

Jacqueline recoiled as though she'd been slapped. "Well, of course not," she tittered. "It's just that, well, you don't want to be stuck raising a child on your own. Do you?"

Obviously she wouldn't be getting any "help" from her boss. "I'll manage."

Jacqueline stared at her as though seeing her for the first time. "But your career, your job? How will you—?"

"I'll manage," Terri repeated. "And I'll train a replacement. You won't even know I'm gone." She would simply explain to that poor, unfortunate soul that all she—or he—had to do was to think of herself as a nonentity, and she would get along with Jacqueline just fine. *It always worked for me…until now.*

With that obstacle overcome, Terri went on with life as usual— until she heard the latest rumor at the coffee pot.

"Why didn't you tell me you were pregnant?" Constance demanded. "I should have been the first to know!"

"You were." She'd made the "butterball" crack long before anyone else knew about it. Terri simply hadn't confirmed the cause.

"I was not!" she said, stomping her foot. "I heard it from Darcy in personnel."

"That's a HIPAA violation, I believe," Terri said with a frown. "I should report her."

"Don't you dare!" she warned. "I get all the best gossip from her. Including a little something about your boss, although I'm not sure how she knows it. I mean, it's not like she had to fill out a form—yet."

Her expression dared Terri not to ask, so she didn't. Constance told her anyway. Her voice dropped to a hoarse whisper. "Her husband is suing her for divorce!" She wriggled like a delighted puppy. "Can you believe it?"

Terri believed it, all right. What she found hard to believe was that he hadn't done it *years* ago.

"Oh, and get this." Hunching her shoulders, she pressed a hand to her lips, barely able to contain her excitement. "He's claiming abandonment and mental cruelty!"

The mental cruelty Terri could understand. Jacqueline was mentally cruel to nearly everyone. But abandonment? If she'd abandoned him, she couldn't very well be mentally cruel to him, could she? The two would cancel each other out because with Jacqueline, "abandonment" would be an act of pure benevolence. "I don't get it."

"No sex and they aren't living together," Constance replied promptly. "Can you imagine being married to a beautiful woman like Jacqueline and never getting any? I think that's pretty damned cruel."

Terri knew the gist of it was true, and she could see the cruelty part, she just couldn't quite see it as abandonment. It wasn't as though he couldn't take care of himself. "That sounds pretty weak."

Constance shrugged. "He wanted a divorce, and she wouldn't agree to it. He's just looking for a way out. Apparently that was the best he could do."

While this was true, Terri could have easily supplied Jacqueline with excellent grounds for divorce if *she'd* wanted a way out—which she apparently didn't. But Ben? Terri knew that if she were to come clean, Jacqueline would have a whole lot more to throw in his face. Things could get really nasty.

How badly did he want out of the marriage? Would he be willing to risk losing everything? Terri didn't know much about divorce laws, but somehow she felt that adultery would carry more weight than some kind of de facto separation, which, in actuality, was all it was. If it ever went to court, the outcome was anyone's guess. But Terri's testimony could only benefit Jacqueline, and she'd much rather be on the other side.

No, the best she could do for Ben was to continue to keep quiet about the identity of her child's father. Once the dust settled and the divorce was over with, she might tell him—or she might not. Ben might prefer to go out and find another woman to marry. Perhaps he'd already found one, although Terri doubted that she was the one he'd found. He'd never said anything about love or marriage. In fact, the only thing he'd said was that he would have liked the white stain on her shirt better if he'd been the one to put it there. Not, "I love you, and I wish it had been me."

He'd only been annoyed because Terri's two boyfriends were getting plenty of action and he wasn't. He must have figured that Terri was promiscuous enough that she wouldn't mind if he climbed into bed with her. He was only half right, but even so, it wasn't quite that simple.

Oddly enough, Terri's out-of-wedlock pregnancy seemed to give all sorts of men the idea that she *was* promiscuous. Even Roger—the scuzzball with a dick the length of Constance's index finger—started hitting on her. Terri was putting paper in the copier one afternoon, when he sidled up behind her and casually ran his hand over her buns.

"I'm really surprised to see you knocked up, Terri," he murmured. "I didn't think you liked men."

Terri straightened up and edged away from him. "I don't." Although she did like one—well, *three*—of them. Roger wasn't on the list. He was…sleazy. Aside from the fact that he was a shit-head.

"I like pregnant women," Roger went on, covering the distance she'd put between them. The carnal gleam in his eyes made her take another step back. "I like how their tits get bigger. You've always had a pretty nice rack on you, but now…well, they're making my dick hard all the time."

What would a dick the length of a woman's finger look like when it was hard? A Magic Marker, perhaps? Or would it be more along the lines of a Sharpie? No, it might resemble the *cap* on a Sharpie, but not the whole thing. Then again, a Sharpie cap wasn't quite as long as an index finger. It crossed her mind to ask him to show it to her, just out of curiosity, but she didn't want to give him the wrong idea.

Now cornered between the file cabinet and the wall, Terri realized just how inexperienced she was and made a mental note to never let it happen again. *Always maintain an escape route.*

Roger pressed his groin against her body and thrust his hips forward. "Want to feel it?"

To be perfectly honest, Terri didn't feel much of anything and shook her head.

"Maybe you'd rather suck it," he went on, still grinding his nonexistent dick against her. "I like naked women with big tits down on their knees sucking my dick. Makes me want to come in their face."

While this was something Terri liked, somehow she felt that Roger's emissions wouldn't have quite the same effect as Chris's had. His were like sweet cream, whereas Roger's cum was probably more like vinegar.

"Come on, Terri," he growled. "Put my hard rod in your mouth and suck it. You know you want to."

That's it! Pretzel rods! Broken pretzel rods! That's what his penis would look like! Terri began laughing hysterically, and, as an afterthought, gave him a knee in the groin to remember her by. She returned to her desk laughing so hard she nearly wet her panties. If that was sexual harassment, she figured she could deal with it. Roger wasn't her boss, though. He was just another stupid peon, which put his behavior more along the lines of lateral violence. Then she remembered the jalapeños she'd had on her hamburger at lunch and decided that perhaps she *should* have sucked him. *No, not worth the effort.* She wasn't sure he'd be able to feel the heat anyway. The fire on her tongue had about gone by then. Maybe she ought to keep a jar of them handy should the need ever arise again. The thought that he might not be able to "arise" again for quite a while got her laughing all over again.

She considered sharing that little episode with Constance, but since she hadn't bothered to relate any of her other—and infinitely better—stories, she didn't see the point. She was still slightly miffed at Constance for the butterball comment, anyway.

Jacqueline never mentioned her divorce, which was odd considering her role in the Myrtle Beach adventure. On the other hand, Terri had already heard enough negative comments about Ben, and any words spoken in his defense would have undoubtedly aroused Jacqueline's suspicions. That was one little seed of knowledge Terri had no desire to plant in her mind.

About the only thing Jacqueline did do was to ask Terri to get rid of the picture of Ben that had been sitting on her desk for so many years. Obviously, she didn't feel the need to pretend anymore and wanted him out of her sight.

Terri not only took the wedding photograph, but also scanned it and backed it up on two different thumb drives. After deleting Jacqueline's image, she made multiple prints, if for no other reason than to be able to show them to her child. She put them in her wallet, desk drawer, and even on the inside of her medicine cabinet at home. She didn't care that it was an older picture and that he'd aged since then. It was still a picture of Ben, and, therefore, something to be cherished.

Terri began to realize that once the divorce was final and he was out of Jacqueline's life forever, he would also be out of hers. She would never see him again. That thought was almost too much to bear until she reminded herself that his son or daughter might at least look a little bit like him. Unfortunately, that tiny scrap of hope didn't console her very much.

ℰℛ

Life drifted on in much the same way it always had. Jacqueline became embroiled various new crises and Terri somehow managed to resolve them. Summer became autumn and the leaves began to fall. The man at the hot dog stand wore a jacket and then a coat and before long, it was Christmas. The beach, the ocean, purple bikinis, and virile young men seemed so long ago and far away as to never have existed at all. It had taken several months, but Terri had finally come to the conclusion that her biggest mistake was in not telling Ben how she felt about him. It probably wouldn't matter now, but if she'd only opened her mouth and actually said the words, things might have turned out differently.

Christmas shopping was tougher than usual. Instead of searching for the perfect gifts for her family, she kept catching herself trying to figure out what to get for Ben. The trouble was, she knew so little about him, it was impossible to know what he might like.

She was miserable. Having always been on a fairly even keel before, being down in the dumps was a new experience. After a while, she couldn't even eat all her poppers when she got them because she cried too much. She felt alone in a way she never had before. The guys had ruined her. She wasn't satisfied with only herself for company anymore, but there was no one else she wanted to be with. Except Ben, and he obviously didn't want any part of her. He knew *exactly* where to find her and he hadn't even bothered. She would have given a million dollars if Chris or Joey had shown up on her doorstep. She missed them so much it hurt, but she didn't even know their last names.

It wasn't the sex she missed, either. It was the companionship, which was something Terri had never needed before.

But she certainly needed it now.

⁊⊃Cℛ

Ben was furious. Jackie had missed two court dates now, and he was sick of it. Opting for a face-to-face confrontation, he spent some time waiting for the right moment, managing to catch her alone in her office just as she returned from lunch. He'd hoped to find her office empty so he could be waiting at the door for her, but this was even better, although he still couldn't shake the notion that, as

Jackie's assistant, Terri might feel enough loyalty to try to keep him at bay. Thankfully, she wasn't there to ward him off. If he'd had to bull his way past her, he wasn't sure he could've done it.

Jackie stood behind her desk, rummaging through her purse when Ben entered her office, closing the door behind him. "Hello, Jackie. Been to any good divorce hearings lately?"

She was still beautiful, still in control, with only an expression of mild surprise to reveal any emotion whatsoever. "Why, Ben! What on earth are you doing here?"

He snorted a laugh. "I think that's fairly obvious."

This time, she didn't bother to feign ignorance. "Can I help it if I had to miss those court dates?"

"Maybe, but I think you skipped them on purpose. Why are you doing this? If it's about the money—"

"It's not about the money," she snapped.

"Well, then what is it? You don't want me. You never have. I just wish it hadn't taken me so many years to see past your lies and discover the truth."

Her chin went up and her whole body stiffened. "I don't know what you're talking about. I've done my best for our marriage, and you know it."

Ben shook his head. "You don't get it, do you? It's *over.* You can stop pretending you care anything about me or our marriage. But I would like to know one thing. Why?"

"Why, what?" She attempted to pin him to the wall with that steely-eyed look he knew so well. It didn't work this time.

"Why you insist on continuing this farce when you know you don't love me and probably never have?"

She stiffened even further. "We're married. Until death do us part. Remember?"

Ben laughed mirthlessly. "Oh, I remember the vows, and I also remember something about promising to love, honor, and cherish, which is something you never did." He paused, raking a hand through his hair. "I tried. I really did. But if you think what we have is love, you're even more heartless than I thought."

"You will *not* make me the scapegoat in this divorce."

"Oh, so that's it. I forgot. You don't like to lose, do you? Mind telling me why you married me in the first place? Women don't need to be married in this day and age, and you sure as hell didn't marry me for sex."

Her gaze never wavered but her reply was as evasive as ever. "I had my reasons."

"If you'd wanted a marriage of convenience, you might have at least mentioned that to me in the beginning. I'm sure we could've found an illegal immigrant who needed a green card."

"If I'd wanted an illegal immigrant, I'd have married one," she spat back. "Do you *really* want to know why I married you?"

"Absolutely." He sat down on the edge of her desk. The flick of her brow was the only sign she'd noticed this infraction, but Ben knew it for what it was. Irritation. *Good.*

"I married you because I felt sorry for you. You had a good future, but you were so damned ugly, I knew you'd never find a wife."

"Nice try," Ben said with a smirk. "I may be ugly, but you've never felt sorry for anyone in your life. I think you married me because you had something to hide."

Her eyes flashed with anger, but she still had herself under control. "You're delusional."

"No, I don't think so. Got a girlfriend on the side?"

Ben had the pleasure of seeing Jackie's face flush—the one reaction she couldn't control. "I am *not* a lesbian."

Ben shrugged. "Didn't think so. That was just a shot in the dark. You have no feelings toward either sex. You only wanted to make it look like you did."

The change in her voice was barely perceptible. "I have feelings."

"Yeah, right. Bad feelings, maybe. But that's all. No, I'm thinking you wanted to be married so other men wouldn't bother you. Sexually, I mean. Obviously *everyone* bothers you in some way."

"That's not true," she protested.

"Oh, of course it isn't," Ben mocked. "But if that's the case, then why don't you tell me what *is* true? I might even believe you."

"Get out of my office." She hadn't cracked yet, but she was about to.

Ben shook his head. "Nope."

"Get out or I'll call Security and have you *thrown* out."

Ben scratched his head. "That wouldn't be very good for your image, would it?"

"You don't give a *damn* about my image. If you did, you wouldn't be here pushing a divorce on me. Unless of course you've got some little slut you want to make an honest woman of."

Ben started to retort that Terri was *not* a slut, until he remembered that Jackie couldn't possibly know there had been anything between the two of them—unless Terri had told her.

No. If she had, Jackie would have used it against him in the divorce, and Ben refused to have Terri's name dragged through the mud. He would keep her out of this mess until it was over and done with.

He got up from her desk and stared at her for a moment, shaking his head. She was so pathetic he almost felt sorry for her. "You wouldn't know an honest woman if she kicked you in the ass."

୫ଓଃ

Terri had just returned to the office after lunch on one of her more miserable days when she heard the unmistakable sounds of an argument taking place in Jacqueline's office, which was odd because Jacqueline rarely argued with anyone. *Looks like she couldn't get even, so she finally got mad.* Terri didn't give a damn. She set her purse down on the desk and had just removed her coat when the door to Jacqueline's office flew open and Ben stormed out.

Terri's gasp of surprise must have caught his attention, for he did see her, his swift glance registering recognition before becoming an angry glare as he ran his eyes over her pregnant belly. If Terri had imagined that he would be overjoyed at the sight of her, she was doomed to disappointment, for he swept right past her without a word.

She was still staring after him as he strode toward the elevator when the whole world faded to black.

Chapter 19

"Oh, just shut up and get away from her, you fuckin' asshole!" Constance snapped.

Groaning, Terri opened her eyes and saw that it was not Ben who Constance was calling an asshole, but Roger. *I should have known.*

"She doesn't need your grubby little fingers groping her, so back off!"

"I was just checking for a pulse!" Roger exclaimed. "C'mon, Constance! Lighten up!"

Constance slapped his hand away. "You're supposed to check for a pulse at the wrist or the throat, not on the chest—or weren't you paying attention in CPR class?"

"Well, b-breathing, then," he sputtered. "I wanted to see if she was breathing."

"What you *wanted* was to feel her up," Constance said. "I've seen you staring at her tits. Go on, get lost. I'll handle this."

"Oh, all right," Roger grumbled as got to his feet. "A guy can't even *try* to be chivalrous around here…"

Chivalry. The mere word brought to mind the last time a man had held Terri while he tried to console her, and because it was Chris, her tears began to flow in earnest. Chris had held her while she cried, and then Joey had kissed her in the shower. Both of those times she'd needed consoling because Ben had left her without a word. It felt even worse this time because now she had that awful look on his face to remember. She almost wished she hadn't seen him. *Almost.*

"It's okay, Terri," Constance said, apparently misinterpreting the reason for her sobs. "He didn't really do that much to you. I got here in time. I guess Big Bad Ben scared you, huh?"

Since this was as good an excuse as any, Terri nodded her agreement. Expectant mothers were prone to all sorts of strange symptoms. Fainting at the sight of an angry man probably wasn't as odd as it seemed.

Constance helped her into her chair, at which point Roger might have actually been of some use, but he was cowering over by the main reception desk.

"Stay there," Constance said firmly. "I'll be right back."

Within moments, she returned and applied ice wrapped in a paper towel to Terri's forehead. She was so swift and efficient, Terri had to assume she'd done it before. Constance had done *lots* of things before, it seemed. *Unlike me.* "Ever done it with two guys at once?"

"What? You mean sex? With two guys? At the same time? No. That would be too kinky."

So Constance did, indeed, have her limits. Limits that Terri had exceeded on her first time at bat. No wonder Ben had looked at her like that. He probably thought the same thing.

Constance gazed at her curiously. "Why do you ask?"

"Nothing. Just checking is all." Terri sat up straighter and took a deep breath. "Speaking of which, I should check on Jacqueline. She might need something."

"Yeah, like her head examined!" Constance exclaimed. "That husband of hers is a real hottie! No way would I ever kick him out of bed!"

Terri wouldn't have, either, and that was aside from the fact that he had a really nice dick. "A bit of a hot head, though," she admitted. Both of them were, actually.

"Well, who could blame him?" Constance said. "How on earth did he ever get mixed up with her, anyway?"

"Beats the shit out of me," Terri replied. After struggling to her feet, she went over and knocked on Jacqueline's door. Opening it a crack, she peeked inside. Jacqueline was on the telephone and was actually smiling as she glanced up to dismiss Terri with a quick nod.

Quite obviously she was in the process of getting even.

Poor Ben! What devious little plan did Jacqueline have up her sleeve now? An open phone book had been sitting on her desk. Who would she call? Another lawyer? Surely she had the current one on speed dial by now. Or perhaps not. Terri had shown her how to program the phone—more than once—but she might have forgotten. It didn't matter. None of this was Terri's business. Not anymore.

She went on with her day; sent out memos, answered the phone fifty million times, scheduled appointments, and spent the rest of the time organizing the files on one of the new ad campaigns. In short, she did her best to put Ben out of her mind. He kept creeping back in, though, torturing her until she reached the conclusion that being hung up on a guy who not only disliked, but hated you, really sucked. *Big ones.*

She was putting on her coat to leave that evening, thinking of stopping off for some chicken lo mein when her brain finally came up with an idea. Jacqueline had been on the phone hiring a hit man! No, that was stupid. Hired guns didn't advertise in the Yellow Pages.

But private investigators did.

Jacqueline was looking for dirt on Ben, which made Terri wonder if there was any to find—aside from his involvement with her. No one could have possibly known anything about that except Joey and Chris, and they were pretty well untraceable—or were they?

Terri had no idea what a private investigator might be able to discover, but she couldn't see that anyone could tie her baby to Ben without a blood test or a confession. Jacqueline had no grounds to suspect that Terri and Ben had ever been intimate, although she *did* know they'd spent two nights in the same room together. She had even suggested it...

That being the case, Terri knew she should never even attempt to talk to Ben—at least not until the divorce was final. If he was being watched, it wouldn't take a genius to figure out the rest of it if they were ever seen together. She couldn't even list him as the father on the baby's birth certificate—which she had fully intended to do. No, her best course of action was to keep her mouth shut and stay out of everyone's way. If subpoenaed, she would have to tell the truth, the whole truth, and nothing but the truth, but she certainly didn't have to volunteer any information until then.

ಬಂಡ

Unfortunately, Ben must not have been thinking quite as clearly as Terri because she had no sooner left the building that evening when he suddenly appeared at her side, hooking a firm arm through hers.

"I see one of your boyfriends got a little careless." His voice sounded hard and bitter as he propelled her forward along the sidewalk. "What's the matter, couldn't you find them to go crying to when you found out you were pregnant?"

"They didn't—" Terri began to protest their innocence, but he cut her off.

"Oh, never mind," he said irritably. "What the devil is Jacqueline up to now? She's been stalling the divorce for weeks."

Terri took a deep breath and tried for a calm, steady tone. "I don't know, but you need to let go of me. *Right now.*"

"What's the matter? Forgotten how much you liked being manhandled?" She could hear the sneer in his voice.

Knowing she probably deserved it, Terri let that one pass. "You shouldn't be seen with me."

"Why not?" He let out a mirthless little laugh. "Do you think she'll try to pin that baby of yours on me? I notice you haven't tried it, so I can only assume you don't think it's mine. Look, all I want are some answers, and I'm sure as hell not getting them from Jackie." He paused, running a hand through his hair. "I'm so sick of all the drama. I suppose it's all my fault for wanting to be a normal, average guy with a wife, two kids, and a house in the country, but it doesn't look like I'll ever get there, does it?"

"You can work on that after the divorce," Terri said quietly. "Isn't that why you're doing this?"

He blew out a pent-up breath. "Shit, I don't know. Seems like I don't know anything anymore."

"Listen, Ben, Jacqueline is my boss, and I don't want to end up losing my job over this. I have a child to think about now—and no husband to help me—so job security is more important than ever, but I'll tell you this much." She lowered her voice a notch. "Watch your back." She carefully removed his hand from her arm and moved away. "And please, don't ever try to talk to me again."

Terri picked up her pace and never looked back. Dodging through the throng of people on the street, she did her best to put as much space and as many other bodies between her and Ben as she possibly could. Breathing hard, she prayed to all the saints in heaven that Jacqueline hadn't done what she suspected in hiring an investigator—but she had a strong feeling it wouldn't help very much.

Jacqueline was completely ruthless. She would do whatever it took to come through the divorce looking like the innocent party, and she wouldn't give a damn who she took down in the process. Terri, on the other hand, simply refused to hand over the proof of adultery that would make Ben's abandonment and mental cruelty charges look like a joke. Everyone could go right on thinking her baby was anyone's but Ben's.

She kept walking and didn't stop until she'd locked the door to her apartment behind her. There was absolutely no one for her to trust or to confide in. She hadn't even told her family the truth. Her mother had already chalked it up to Terri's enigmatic personality. Her sister called her Rosemary, as in *Rosemary's Baby*. Terri was not only miffed because that particular reference would make Ben the devil, but, as the movie buff of the family, she was also surprised that her sister knew anything about a forty-year-old film. Her father was a taciturn, practical sort of man whose only suggestion was that she should buy savings bonds.

Terri wished with all her heart that she had a way of contacting Chris and Joey, because she could at least have talked to them about this mess, but an investigator might have been able to trace her phone records, so perhaps it was best that she couldn't. She still missed them terribly and wondered if any of their other women had missed them quite as much. They'd been so sweet, and she longed for the warmth of their bodies surrounding her while she slept.

She might have missed those two, but she missed Ben a helluva lot more—and it didn't matter whether he hated her or not. If only *he* was the one she worked with rather than Jacqueline. That way, she would at least get to see him on a regular basis, and he might even see his child now and then. He probably wouldn't know it was his, although the possible resemblance might have been enough to make him wonder.

How strange it was that Ben would assume Chris and Joey had been the ones to be careless, especially when he was the one who hadn't bothered to use any form of birth control. Deciding that he wasn't the father just because Terri hadn't chosen to inform him was a bit ridiculous. She'd seen plenty of movies with that story line, but perhaps he hadn't seen the same films that she had. Still, he should have known better, just as he should have known better than to get mixed up with Jacqueline. Even Joey had pegged her as one to avoid—although his own choice of words on the subject had been much more colorful—*a nutcracker if I ever saw one!*

Joey was smarter than most people. He knew what he liked and what he didn't, and on a gut level, he could be every bit as insightful as Chris—as long as no one asked him to figure out the square root of nine. Terri considered the ability to recognize a man-killer to be a far more useful skill. Too bad she hadn't been able to recognize what a lady-killer Ben was from his photograph. If she had, she probably would've faked a heart attack rather than set foot in that airport.

ℰℛ

In keeping with his determination to steer clear of Terri until his divorce from Jackie was final, Ben had practically had to tie his fingers together to keep from calling her. He'd somehow managed to keep his distance even though he knew exactly where to find her. As a result, he hadn't laid eyes on her since the night he'd left Myrtle Beach. It never occurred to him that she might have been expecting a child.

Ben was no judge of such things, but if he had to guess, he'd have said that she was at least six months along. His first assumption was that one of those boys in Myrtle Beach had gotten her pregnant, which was bad enough. His next thought was that she'd married one of them, which was even worse.

He left the building and started walking, but kept ending up right back where he started. When he finally spotted her, his pent up anger had reached the boiling point. He'd been nasty and rough with a pregnant girl—an *unmarried* pregnant girl, as it turned out—whom he loved with all his heart, but who clearly never wanted to speak to him again.

She *had* told him to watch his back, though, which meant that Jackie was plotting something. Not that Jackie's plots were anything new. He'd been watching his back for years.

What if Jackie knew something he didn't? Did she know he'd climbed into Terri's bed?

No. If she knew that, she would've thrown it in his face every chance she got. That was just about the only dirt she'd be able to find on him too. He didn't have a girlfriend or anything else she could use against him.

Then it hit him, stopping him dead in his tracks. Terri hadn't accused him of being the baby's father, nor had she disagreed when he made the assumption that he wasn't, but those two boys had known exactly what they were doing and what they were getting into. Ben had been the one acting like an impulsive teenager, not them. They'd probably used condoms. He hadn't.

The baby is mine.

The surge of joy that accompanied that thought robbed him of breath, but though having a baby with Terri was exactly what he wanted, the timing couldn't have been worse.

Pedestrians flowed around Ben like creek water around a boulder, some muttering their annoyance, but most ignoring him. As his breathing steadied, he began to sort out the possibilities. For the past six months he'd berated himself for his behavior that night. He should have known better than to lose control, should've considered the consequences, but he hadn't given them a thought. Terri hadn't seemed like the type to sleep around when he'd met her in the airport. Now she was pregnant. If he'd given it any thought at all, which he hadn't, he would have known that the child was his.

And so would Terri, but why wouldn't she tell him?

The answer was obvious. She didn't want Jackie to find out because she was afraid of losing her job. Terri didn't know he loved her. And why would she? He'd never made her any promises or given her any reason to believe that he would come riding up on a white horse once his divorce was final. That and the fact that right after he'd made love to her, he'd packed up and disappeared from her life.

She probably thought he hated her. He'd left Jackie's office wearing an expression of complete and utter disgust, and when he'd spotted Terri, he'd felt a surge of anger and jealousy that had nearly driven him mad. Terri probably assumed it was aimed at her.

I am so *screwed...*

Chapter 20

A few weeks passed with no news whatsoever. Terri wasn't as up on the office gossip as Constance, but even *she* didn't seem to know anything. If that investigator—if there actually was one—had come up with anything useful, no one ever heard a peep. Terri felt like she was in a holding pattern, endlessly circling the airport, waiting for permission to land, all the while knowing that a crash was imminent.

Jacqueline was the same as ever. Ben never made another appearance in the office and Terri thought she might actually be getting over him. She only thought about him once a minute instead of every second that ticked by. She told herself repeatedly that she didn't care about him, but she knew it was a lie.

One day during her lunch hour, she was walking past Starbucks and there he was, sitting by the window and reading a newspaper. If he'd taken to going there just to keep tabs on Jacqueline, he was doomed to failure. Anytime the boss got a Caffè Mocha, Terri was the one who picked it up.

She also spotted him across the street one evening as she was walking home, but she didn't think he saw her. Actually, she didn't think he'd seen her either time and wondered why she should be noticing him on the street when she never had before. It could have been because she'd only seen a photograph of him before, but New York was a pretty big place. Finding your best friend in a crowd wasn't always easy.

It wasn't until she noticed him in the subway while on her way to a prenatal visit that she realized she was being followed. Which was sort of funny, really, because if he had a private detective following him, then that made three of them following each other around New York. She chuckled to herself thinking that they should quit the sneaking around and have lunch together so they could all relax. Unfortunately, if there truly *was* an investigator on Ben's tail, she couldn't very well confront him. So, she went on seeing him but never speaking, and he got closer and closer with each passing day.

ℕℛ

On a Friday afternoon in mid-December, Terri was waiting in line at Starbucks for Jacqueline's infamous Caffè Mocha when he came up to stand behind her. "I see Jackie is still hooked on that stuff."

Terri nodded, opting not to turn around. "I thought I told you to stay away from me."

"Yes, you did. Forgive me for not listening."

"You're *supposed* to be watching your back."

"Oh, I am," he said carelessly. "The private dick is across the street. I think I managed to give him the slip this time. He thinks I'm still in the drugstore."

She started to turn toward the pharmacy on the corner, but caught herself in time. "So, there is one, then?"

"Oh, yeah," he replied. "And I'll give him this much, he's persistent."

The line moved forward. So did Ben. "Why are *you* so persistent? I see you everywhere. Are you following me?"

"Yep," he replied.

"Why?"

"You tell me," he said. "If your two boyfriends weren't careless, then it must have been someone else, and I never see you with anyone. Who is it?"

"Who is what?" Terri asked, stalling.

"Your baby's father. I have the strangest feeling I might have a stake in this."

"Oh? And what makes you think that?"

His breath tickled the back of her neck when he laughed,

making her acutely aware of just how close he was. "I seem to recall fucking you once, and while I assumed at the time that you must have been on the Pill or you wouldn't have been messing around with those two young punks, it could be that I was wrong."

"So?"

"So, if that's my baby you're carrying, I think I should know about it."

"Aren't you afraid your wife will be able to accuse you of adultery and take everything you've got?"

"She's already got most of it," he replied. "A little more won't matter."

"Then why all the sneaking around? Why not just come right out and ask me?"

"It's more fun this way, don't you think? No, really. I don't want to give her detective the chance to find out first. I don't want you losing your job—at least not until I'm sure."

"Pardon me if I fail to see the difference. I think I lose out either way."

"Not necessarily," he said. "So, is it?"

"Is it what?"

He growled in her ear, sending tingles skittering across her neck. "Come on, Terri, you're not that stupid. Is it mine?"

"Caffè Mocha, please," she said to the clerk—the cute one. Dark hair, green eyes, nice hands. If she'd learned anything on her summer vacation, it was to appreciate an attractive man when she saw one. Unfortunately, the most attractive man in the building was standing behind her. Turning her head slightly, she aimed a jibe over her shoulder. "How should I know? It was dark."

"Yes, it was," he said smugly. "But I still knew it was you. You drove me insane from the first moment I saw you. You didn't know that, did you? One glance and I felt like something hit me right in the nuts. I knew you were the one, Terri. I knew it then, and I still know it now. Nothing has changed."

The boy handed over Jacqueline's coffee. Terri paid him with a shaking hand and turned to leave.

Ben stuck to her like a cocklebur. "I'm going to follow you home, tonight, Terri. And I'm going to do my damnedest to give Jackie all the dirt on me she wants. I want this divorce to happen, and I don't give a shit if I have to pay through the nose for the rest of my life. I want you, Terri. And I'm going to get you."

Terri could scarcely believe what she was hearing. His tone wasn't the least bit romantic, so why were her knees getting weak? Despite a slight wobble, she kept right on walking toward the door. However, in her haste to reach it, she tripped over a little old lady's purse and nearly fell, coming down hard on her left foot, which gave way beneath her. White-hot knives of pain pierced her ankle just as Ben caught her, but instead of helping her to a chair, he kept her hopping on one foot all the way out the door.

"Stop!" she gasped when they reached the sidewalk. "I'm hurt, you idiot!"

"I know." He scooped her up in his arms. "I think I can carry you back to the office. You're not very heavy."

Terri was concentrating so hard on not spilling Caffè Mocha all over the two of them that she didn't bother with the obvious comment on how heavy she'd gotten since the last time he'd held her in his arms. *Feels nice, though.*

Ben glanced across the street. "Jesus Christ! That dumb ass is still waiting outside the drugstore! Dammit, he should be getting pictures of this!" He stopped and blew out an exasperated breath. "I wonder if I should wave at him."

"Oh, please don't," Terri begged. "You might drop me."

"Good point." He tapped his foot. "Maybe I should just stand here kissing you until a crowd gathers. He's sure to notice us, then."

"Does he *have* to see us?" She didn't mind being seen kissing Ben, but she preferred to kiss him in private.

"Not really." Ben turned and strode off towards the agency building. "I'll just carry you back to the office, tell Jackie that I knocked up her assistant, and then she'll fire you so we can go home. Then I can try knocking you up all over again."

"My, how romantic!" If he noticed the sarcasm, he chose to ignore it.

"Isn't it though?" he said happily. "It's like the end of *An Officer and a Gentleman,* only in reverse."

Terri had to think about that for a minute. *Let's see now… Richard Gere carried whatsherface out of the factory, presumably to marry her and then have lots of little officers. Yes, he's right. It* is *that scene in reverse.* Terri was already pregnant, and they were going back to the factory, except for one teensy little detail. "You aren't in uniform," she pointed out.

"Picky, picky, picky…" He stepped off the curb and crossed the street. "You *do* love me, don't you? That night, when I said I wanted that spot on your shirt to be mine, and you said 'me too,' that's what you meant, wasn't it?"

"Well, no," Terri replied. "I only meant I wanted to suck your dick."

"Oh." He sounded terribly disappointed, which probably served him right.

Terri thought she should make him squirm just a bit. "So, if you love me so much, why did you leave without a word?"

"Because I'd just done something I'd sworn I would never do! I cheated on my wife—and with her own assistant, no less—while she was asleep in the next room. You know, between you, Jackie, and Tweedle Dum and Tweedle Dee, I was about to lose my mind. A guy can only take so much." He stopped at the next corner and waited for the light to change. "And you, why didn't you tell me you were pregnant? You could have called me. God knows you must have my phone number there somewhere."

"You left town in the middle of the night after having sex with me," she reminded him. "I didn't think you ever wanted to see me again."

"It wasn't that. I was just too fucked up to know *what* to do. Leaving seemed the best choice at the time. I needed to cool off for a while."

Terri was within a hairsbreadth of pouring Jacqueline's coffee down his back. "That happened several months ago. I'd have thought you could cool off quicker than that."

"Well, Jackie is partly responsible for the timing," he grumbled. "If she'd granted me a divorce, I would have said something sooner. But it took too long, and then when I saw you were expecting and hadn't said anything to me, I figured it was someone else's baby."

"Got a bit pissed, didn't you?"

"I was already pretty mad," he admitted. "That just clinched it."

She was trying very hard not to smile and failing miserably. "Still mad?"

"Not especially." He leaned closer and kissed her. She felt the tingles all the way to her sore ankle. "Do you really love me?"

"Yeah."

"That's all you have to say?"

Terri tried for a bit more animation. "Well, yeah!"

"Guess I'll have to get used to that," he said with a sigh. "Do you think you could possibly say more than two words to me at a time?"

"Probably. I've done it lots of times. You only notice the times when I don't say much." Terri glanced over his shoulder as a sudden movement caught her eye. "What's the private eye look like?"

"Tall, bald, black mustache, big shoulders," he replied. "Brown coat and blue shirt today. Why?"

"He's spotted us."

"What makes you think that?"

"He's running after us with a camera."

"I should stop, then," Ben said. "I could use a bit of a breather, anyway." He moved closer to a building and stood beneath the awning.

Terri glanced up at the sky as the first swirling flake touched her nose. Then another one melted on her glasses. "Put me down."

"Nope, don't want to." He sounded quite cheerful. "I like you right where you are. Besides, I want a picture of this."

"Okay." Terri didn't really want him to put her down, either, but she didn't want him to hurt his back.

"So, what do you think?" he asked. "Should we be facing toward him or away from him?"

"You're the one he's following," she said after careful consideration. "You should be facing him."

"Yeah, right." Ben turned slightly and leaned up against the brick wall. "How's this?"

"Perfect," Terri replied. "Now he can see us both. Should I smile at him?"

Ben's eyebrow lifted suggestively and he leaned closer. "How about kissing me?"

"In a minute," she said, pushing his head away with her fingertips. "If I kiss you, he won't be able to see your face."

"Oh, well, then, let him get a couple of shots, and *then* kiss me."

"Actually, I think I'd rather stick my tongue out at him."

"That's a nice touch," he conceded. "But kiss me first."

Terri leaned in and planted a big juicy one right on his lips. "You don't kiss as well as Joey."

"Too bad. Kiss me anyway."

So she did. "Your lips are too hard," she complained. "Make them softer, like they've melted."

"Like this?" he asked, and then tried again.

"Better, but still not as good as Joey." Joey would have to go down as the all-time best kisser. "Haven't had much practice, have you?"

"Not lately," he admitted. "You'll have to coach me."

"Oh, I know all kinds of things now," she said proudly. "Joey and Chris taught me everything they could think of."

He grimaced. "I think I'd like to rip their dicks off."

"I'd much rather you didn't," Terri said with a shudder. "Their dicks aren't as nice as yours, but that's no reason to rip them off.

Besides, I have no idea where they live, which is probably a good thing." She thought Ben should be thanking them, but men were so strange.

"Think he's got enough pictures?"

"Probably." The snow was coming down in big, thick flakes. "We should get going. It's snowing."

"Yeah," he said with a grin and started off down the street again. The private eye followed. "Isn't this romantic? You know, I still can't believe this is real. You *are* going to have my baby, aren't you?

"Yep."

"And you really love me." He was smiling like a complete idiot and sounded a bit like Sally Field accepting her Oscar. Terri was entranced. "The woman I love is carrying my child. It's snowing, my love is in my arms, and we're even having pictures taken. I feel like Jimmy Stewart in *It's a Wonderful Life!*"

"It's cold, though." Actually, Terri's feet were freezing. She would've thought it would have made her ankle hurt less, but it didn't.

"Really?" He still sounded ridiculously cheerful. "I hadn't noticed. Maybe you should drink that coffee."

"I don't like coffee. You should know that."

"Yeah, you're right," he said. "I should know that."

He walked on for another block until they reached the agency building. Terri could've put weight on her foot by then, but she let him carry her anyway since it seemed so important to him. He was still smiling when they got on the elevator, and he didn't set her down even then. He didn't seem to be able to stop smiling even when they entered the office. Terri saw him trying, but the smile kept coming back. This was the way he should be all the time—the way he would have been if life and Jacqueline had treated him better. Terri made herself a promise to try and keep him that way.

"Should we put ice on your ankle?"

He looked so eager, Terri hated to disappoint him, but she was already feeling much better, and since her ankle was already cold, it really didn't need ice. But it seemed so important to him, she couldn't very well say no. "Sure." Then she remembered something. "Let's give Jacqueline her coffee first."

Ben carried her through the door to Jacqueline's office and leaned over so she could set the cup on the desk. Jacqueline was on the telephone at the time and nearly dropped the receiver when they entered.

Ben turned, carried Terri back to her desk, and sat her down gently in her chair. Then he took off her shoe and began massaging her foot and ankle. She looked down at the top of his curly head and smiled. He was *so* adorable.

Constance drifted over, and Ben sent her to get an ice pack. Roger looked as though he wanted to disappear into the woodwork. Terri considered telling him that Ben had a much larger dick than he did, but at the moment, she didn't feel like discussing anatomy. She felt like she'd fallen into a 1930s romantic comedy. Fred and Ginger would be dancing by at any moment, and Cary Grant was waiting at the top of the Empire State Building for Deborah Kerr. Despite feeling a bit Katherine Hepburn-ish herself, Terri seriously doubted that Kate had ever been one to discuss penis size, even with Spencer Tracy—although she could have been wrong about that.

Ben, on the other hand, reminded her more of Charlton Heston, but whether or not he could perform miracles remained to be seen. Then again, after getting the upper hand with the boss from hell, parting the Red Sea ought to be a cinch.

Chapter 21

Unfortunately, it wasn't the 1930s. Everything was in living, breathing color when Jacqueline took the stage for the final scene. She stalked out of her office, her spiked heels practically digging holes in the carpet. She glared at Ben. "What the devil are *you* doing here?"

"Delivering your coffee and your assistant," Ben replied. Terri thought it was remarkable that for once, Jacqueline was angry and Ben wasn't. She liked it much better that way.

Jacqueline glanced at Terri's foot. "What's the matter, Terri? Tripping over things now? Really, Ben, you shouldn't be doing that. That's what she gets for being stupid enough to get so big and pregnant that she can't see her own feet. I don't know why you're bothering with her—or why you're here in my office!"

"I'm not *in* your office," he pointed out. "I'm in *hers.*"

Just then, the private detective got off the elevator and hurried over. He did a double take when he saw Ben and Terri and motioned Jacqueline into her office.

Jacqueline ignored him, her attention still focused on Ben. "Will you get your hands off of her? It's embarrassing." Terri was beginning to understand why Jacqueline tried to avoid getting angry, for at that point, with a red face, bugged out eyes, and pursed lips, she looked like a blushing goldfish. "I never saw such a ridiculous display of solicitude in my life! Look, it's not even swollen!"

"I don't care." Ben went right on massaging Terri's foot and nodded toward the detective. "Why don't you go back in your office and talk to this man? He should have some terrific photos for you. I'd like a few prints myself. Eight by tens, if possible."

Jacqueline ignored that, too. "Really, Ben! I don't see why

you're making such a spectacle of yourself—and over a silly little pregnant girl! I *told* her she should have gotten an abortion. After all, that's what I—"

"Because it's my baby," Ben interjected.

"—did."

In the deafening silence that followed, the two of them stared daggers at one another. Terri suspected that anyone standing between them would have been killed in the crossfire. She'd also found another reason her boss should keep her temper in check—she said some really *stupid* things when she was angry.

Ben let go of Terri's foot and stood up, bearing down on Jacqueline with a deadly intent that had her shrinking back against her private dick. "You had an abortion? *When?"*

Terri had never seen Jacqueline so nonplussed in her life. She lost the goldfish look and turned downright green, then white, and back to red. "Y-you said you d-didn't want any children," she stammered. "So, I—"

"You mean you had an abortion while we were married and didn't tell me?" Ben's tone was ominous. Although she wasn't very well versed in divorce laws, Terri had an idea that this might be even more against the rules than adultery. She made a mental note to Google it as soon as she got the chance.

Jacqueline didn't say a word. Her expression was incriminating enough. Ben looked like he was about to blow a gasket, and Terri considered mentioning the blood pressure issue. Fortunately, the investigator intervened.

Tapping Jacqueline on the shoulder, he didn't seem to notice her slight recoil as he pointed a finger at Ben. "He's the father of her baby. He said it just now in front of witnesses, and I've got pictures to prove it."

Ben laughed. "You think *those* pictures are proof? You should have seen us in Myrtle Beach."

Hoping to settle the matter once and for all, Terri piped up from behind her desk. "He's got a very nice dick. Maybe not the best kisser in the world, but he fucks really well."

A shout of laughter sounded from across the room. Terri was pretty sure it was Constance.

"You didn't!" Jacqueline exclaimed, aghast. "Terri? I don't believe it!"

No, Katherine Hepburn would never say anything like that, but Terri wasn't anything like Kate and never would be. She was a tough little girl from Brooklyn who could say anything she damn well pleased. Starting right *now.*

"Well, why not?" Terri demanded hotly. "You didn't want him—wouldn't even sleep in the same room with him! You even told him to share a room with me! Remember that? Did you think he was a monk? The poor guy just needs a little love and affection, which is something you seem to be incapable of giving to anyone. I've seen you shudder whenever a man tries to get close. You can't stand it. Even your private eye gave you the willies when he tapped you on the shoulder just now."

Jacqueline's face was a total blank—beautiful, yet devoid of life or feeling. She didn't deny any of it.

Terri glanced at Ben. "You wouldn't have wanted a child of yours growing up with her. I mean, talk about your unfit mothers! She's the most selfish person I've ever met." She rounded on Jacqueline again. "Did you think he'd be happy being used as your excuse for not having to fuck your way to the top?"

A quick sweep of the room showed that everyone was waiting breathlessly for her to continue—either that or they were too stunned to pick their chins up off the floor. "I've had to listen to you badmouthing Ben from the very first day I started working here, and I've been hearing it on a regular basis ever since. It's all bullshit. There's nothing wrong with him that a little love won't fix. He's a terrific guy, and he'll be a terrific father. *You're* the one that's screwed up. Just let him go. Because if you don't want him, I *do.*"

Terri paused, taking a deep breath before getting up from her chair. Her ankle was weak, but it held. "And now, I'm tired, pregnant, and it's right before Christmas, and I'm sorry, Jacqueline, but I don't think I can work for you anymore. I'm sick to death of it, and I quit."

Terri slung her purse onto her shoulder just as the entire office erupted with applause and whoops of laughter. Constance started a little office version of The Wave. Roger and another guy gave each other a high five. No, Jacqueline didn't have a fan club—a mutual hatred society, perhaps—but certainly not a fan club.

Ben stood there for a moment, gaping at Terri. "Boy, when you finally decide to talk, you don't pull any punches, do you?"

"Nope."

He glanced at Jacqueline. "Will you *please* show up for the hearing next week?"

Jacqueline looked like she was about to faint as she nodded.

Ben reached out and took Terri's hand. "Will you marry me? Please?"

"Sure."

Ben chuckled, quite obviously pleased with Terri's reply, although he was probably wishing she'd been a bit more elaborate. "Well, that didn't last long, did it?"

"Guess not."

"Think you could say a little more later on?"

"Yep."

"Then let's get out of here."

"You bet."

Ben gathered Terri up in his arms and headed toward the elevator. Although he would have preferred to carry her all the way home, he figured it would be better—and faster—if they took a cab. He noticed several onlookers smiling at them as he carried her through the lobby and out to the street, but he didn't give a damn. Keeping his feelings hidden for so long had worn him out. He didn't care what anyone thought now. All he wanted was to get Terri home and love her for the rest of his life.

After discovering just how quickly New York cabbies would stop to pick up a man carrying an injured woman, he settled Terri in the back seat and then climbed in beside her while she gave the driver her address. The last time he'd been in a car with Terri, they'd barely spoken. He'd been annoyed and she'd been crying. The shy smile she gave him now was much better.

She glanced at the people on the street who'd stopped to stare. "I'll have to remember that ploy the next time I need a cab."

Ben took her hand and raised it to his lips. "That's fine as long as I'm the one who gets to carry you."

She nodded, seeming pleased by this, and her comment was pure Terri. "Okay."

He gave her hand a squeeze with no intention of letting go of it just yet. "I think you need to watch some old movies."

"Old movies?"

"You know, the kind with lots of witty banter between the characters. Might give you some ideas for conversation."

She shook her head. "I watch old movies all the time—that is, when I'm not watching *Star Trek*. I don't think it makes any difference *what* I watch."

"I dunno. That was a pretty long sentence just now—two of them, actually."

"Hey, if you don't like the way I talk—"

"I didn't say that. I don't really mind *how* you talk to me. Just as long as you do."

Her understanding smile did curious things to Ben's heart. "Jacqueline told me you hated getting the silent treatment."

"She should know. She certainly used it on me often enough." Grimacing at the memory, he had a feeling that a much more interesting future lay ahead. "Promise me one thing? Don't clam up on me if you're mad. Just spit it out. Anything's better than not knowing."

"Okay."

Laughing, he slipped an arm around her shoulders and pulled

her up against him. "That was easy."

She nestled closer and sighed, resting her head on his shoulder. "Most things are, as long as you don't try to complicate them."

He nodded his agreement, feeling a surge of warmth as she placed a hand on his chest. "And my relationship with Jackie sure did get complicated."

"No shit. Mind telling me why you stuck it out for so long?"

"I'll be damned if I know. She needed a husband, and I guess I was the one she decided on—don't know why, exactly—and you *know* how it is when she wants something."

Terri snorted a laugh. "I certainly do. Lately I've been leaning toward the idea that she only used your marriage to help her seem more…normal."

"Meaning she's abnormal?" Ben considered this for a moment. "You might be right about that. The funny thing is, she always made me feel like *I* was the abnormal one." He shuddered as he recalled all the times she'd made him feel like an absolute cad for wanting sex, or children, or anything else.

"Don't suppose you've ever read *Rebecca*, have you?"

Puzzled, Ben glanced down at her. "That's an odd question to ask, but no, I haven't."

"It's a classic. You see, Rebecca was this warped woman who was outwardly charming, yet had no heart at all. She married a rich guy—for his money, I suppose—even though she never had any feelings for him—or any other man. She was cold and manipulative, but she was so beautiful she could seduce just about anyone. She only did it so she could laugh at the guys later, and she made her husband's life so miserable that he finally killed her. Of course, she goaded him into it because she was dying of cancer, but *still…*"

Ben cleared his throat with some difficulty. Although he hadn't quite gotten to the point of actually considering murder, if anyone could have driven him to it, it would have been Jackie. "This book…it was fiction. Right?"

"Yes, but there are some definite similarities. You should read it sometime. I think there's a lot of Rebecca in Jacqueline."

Ben shuddered at the thought. "Maybe so, except that Jacqueline doesn't like sex enough to ever seduce anyone."

Terri frowned. "Maybe we should get Chris and Joey to work on her. They might be able to change her mind about all that— although Joey *did* call her a nutcracker. He probably wouldn't want her sucking his balls."

Ben flung up a hand. "I don't want to hear about *them*. I already know I'm not as good a kisser as Tweedle Dum, and I don't want to hear that I don't do it as well as Tweedle Dee. Then again, maybe I'm really *not* any good if Jacqueline was so turned off."

"You do it just fine," Terri said, patting his chest. "I mean, if you'd been the first, it would be different because I wouldn't have known any better, but since I have Chris and Joey to compare—"

Ben's eyes went wide with shock and his voice dropped to a hoarse whisper. "You mean *they* were the first?"

She nodded. "Thanks to you."

"How the hell do you figure that?" he demanded.

"The purple bikini," she replied. "That and the way you were making me see men in a whole new light. You made me realize what I'd been missing. I'd never bothered to look before, and then I took a direct hit from that smile of yours, and…" She stopped there, giving a quick shrug. "I haven't been the same since."

While this revelation warmed the cockles of Ben's heart, something else was bugging him. "Yes, but do you think—that is, I asked you to marry me, and even though you said yes, when it's all said and done, we actually spent only about a day and a half together. Are you sure about this?"

"Pretty sure. I have no problem with living together for a while, though. If I were you, I wouldn't want to run the risk of wasting another ten years on a woman who didn't want me."

"No shit. I still have trouble sorting out how we wound up married. I must've been taken in like everyone else—I *do* need to read that book, by the way. We met during the early planning sessions for a project we were both working on. She was there to get ideas for the ad campaign, and I was doing the preliminary designs for the building. Before I knew it, we were dating and then getting married and everybody was telling me how lucky I was—and it seemed that way—at least at first.

"It was such a gradual thing, the way we drifted apart. One thing led to another, and then one day, I realized I was alone. *Completely* alone, and I didn't like it. I wanted a family, and when I asked her to rethink having kids, she said she would—*think* about it, that is. Turns out she had bigger fish to fry and the idea got dropped. That went on for several years. I would let it slide for a while, then I'd ask again, and she'd put me off." He shook his head sadly, but one glance at Terri's rounded belly made him smile. "I guess you won't be doing that, will you?"

"No," she replied. "And I won't want to live apart, either. I've lived by myself for years and never realized just how lonely I was until I spent that week with you and Chris and Joey. I've missed you an awful lot since then, and, I'll have to admit, I've missed them, too."

"Guess I've got my work cut out for me, trying to replace two of them," he said ruefully.

Terri smiled. "Not really. After all, it took *two* of them to equal *one* of you."

Chapter 22

Ben figured if Terri thought he was worth two other guys whom she seemed to like very well, she must really love him.

The cab stopped outside her apartment building and Ben paid the cabbie and carried her inside, kissing her the whole way. He had to stop long enough to climb the stairs, but as soon as she unlocked her door, he started again. With one quick glance around her living room, he took in the soft beige furniture, antique sewing machine, profusion of house plants, and the pair of Tiffany-style lamps. What set it apart from the typical single woman's apartment was the autographed *Star Wars* poster hanging over the mantelpiece and a scale model of the *Starship Enterprise* on top of the bookcase.

So, I'm marrying a Trekkie…

"Where's your Starfleet uniform?"

Terri sighed and glanced heavenward. "In a plastic bag in my closet."

"Ever wear it?"

She ducked her head as though trying to hide her sheepish smile. "Sometimes. It's autographed, so I don't want to have to wash it."

"Cool. Who've you got?"

"Most of the original cast—the ones who are still living, anyway—and a few of the newer ones."

He gave her another kiss. "You'll have to model it for me sometime."

"Maybe in about six months. Don't think I could fit into it now."

"That's okay. I'd just as soon have you out of it." Ben found her bedroom and laid her down on the bed. About all he noticed in that room was that the bed was a queen and the sheets were blue. "Now that you don't have a job, you can lay around in bed— preferably naked—all the time and give that ankle of yours plenty of time to heal."

"Mmm…sounds nice. But what about you? Don't you have a job you have to go to?" She reached up and tugged at his coat sleeve. "All this time you've been hanging around Starbucks or following me, shouldn't you have been at work?"

Ben pushed off his coat and started working on Terri's. "I took some time off to see if I couldn't get this divorce moving along a little faster. I haven't been able to concentrate very well since our vacation. You've been on my mind constantly, and it wasn't only the sex. That first day on the beach was about as close to heaven as I've ever been."

Terri sighed. "I kinda pretended we were married that day."

"Me too. Want to pretend we're married now?"

"Oh, yeah."

Ben took off her shoes and tried to figure out how to get her out of the rest of her clothes. She was wearing a white long-sleeved turtleneck shirt under a red jumper. "I'm sure this is a very nice, Christmasy outfit, but how the hell do I get you out of it?"

"It all comes off over my head," she replied. "Everything but my panty hose, that is."

"I knew that part." Chuckling, he reached beneath her jumper and found the waistband of her hose and pulled them off. "I probably don't need to take off anything else, anyway."

"Oh, yes you do. If you think that's enough, you've obviously never tried to wear an underwire bra to bed."

"I believe that's a given. Okay then. Everything goes."

Ben's cock had been rock hard all during the cab ride, but by the time he got Terri undressed, it felt like it was on fire. He'd never realized how totally sexy a pregnant woman could be. Her breasts were even larger than before, the areolas dark, the nipples begging to be sucked. He stripped off his own clothes much faster and lay down beside her.

She skimmed a hand over his chest, barely ruffling the trail of curls that led to his groin, making his cock twitch. "Whoa."

"What?"

"You. I didn't get to look at you the last time. It was kinda dark. Remember?"

"I remember." Just having her eyes on his dick was making it drool. "You *are* going to do more than look, aren't you?"

"Oh, yeah."

"And you're going to let *me* do more than look, too, aren't you?"

"Later. I'm going first."

Ben wouldn't have guessed an expectant mother could move that fast, but before he'd taken another breath, she'd spun around and gone down on him. He inhaled sharply as she took him in her mouth, caressing him with her lips and tongue. His own copious fluids mixed with her saliva, allowing a nearly frictionless glide over the head and down his shaft.

He couldn't believe his luck. After a wife who wouldn't even live in the same house with him, he now had Terri, who would not only suck his dick, but actually seemed to enjoy it.

The memory of that night in the hotel was emblazoned on his mind. No woman had ever made him feel the way Terri had. She *wanted* him, and after years of being refused or merely tolerated, the freedom to express his passion for the woman he loved was sheer bliss.

Even though this was not a one-shot deal, he saw no point in saving anything for later or leaving any feelings unexpressed. Not only was his desire for her insatiable, but she was doing him the honor of carrying his child. For that and for her love he would give her anything and everything, holding nothing back.

He would take his turn later, but for now, he let her do as she pleased. Thankful to even be lying in her bed, Ben watched as Terri slid her tongue up to the head and then down to his balls. Her lips nipped at his scrotum, and she moistened the skin with her tongue, proving that what had happened the last time wasn't a fluke or a dream.

"That feels *so* good, Terri. Do you like doing that?"

She sighed, her warm breath ruffling his scrotal hair. "Oh, yeah. Lots."

She must have meant it because she'd actually said three words this time. Obviously three words meant she was opening up. Ben couldn't help but chuckle when it occurred to him that he was also starting to think in shorter sentences. *She's rubbing off on me.* When her subsequent moans and the sudden jackknifing spasms of her body began, he started thinking more along the lines of her *getting* off on him and laughed out loud. "Weren't kidding, were you?"

She backed off briefly. "No. I really do love it. Is that strange?" As if to prove it, she didn't wait for a reply, but sucked a testicle into her mouth.

Ben was sure he'd died and gone to heaven—until she began caressing him with her tongue. Then he realized that analogy was weak. Somehow, he'd wound up in heaven without having to die. "Absolutely not." Groaning, he fisted his hands in the sheets.

Terri let go of him again. "Maybe I should stop that. I don't want this to be over too soon."

Carrying on a conversation while Terri was sucking his nuts was difficult at best, and though Ben hated to discourage her from talking, he was about to explode. He cupped her cheek in his hand, threading his fingers through her hair. "I may not be as good as I used to be, but with you around, I can probably keep going all night."

A raised eyebrow betrayed her skepticism. "Yeah, right. My friend Constance says guys tell her that all the time, but most of them poop out on her. Well…except for this *one* guy, but he was unusual. What's your turnaround time?"

Ben shrugged. "I dunno…ten minutes, maybe?"

Terri gave a little gulp. "Really? That's impressive."

"Hey, back in high school, I didn't have *any* down time. I think it's coming back to me."

"Good." Smiling wickedly, she dipped her head and sucked in his other nut. Ben clutched the sheets and arched his back, spreading his legs wide as he thrust his hips upward. The way things were going, his dick would never be soft again.

Terri grabbed a pillow and stuffed it under his butt. "For better access," she said as she moved around to kneel between his legs.

She wasn't kidding. His dick was sticking straight up, and from that angle, she was able to lick underneath his balls, teasing him until he thought he would fire off the first round into the air.

But Terri had other ideas. She sat back on her heels, and then rocked forward, trapping his cock between her succulent breasts. Ben moaned as she moved, his dick gliding over her warm skin, making soft sucking sounds. Pressing her tits together, she made the fit as tight and slick as if he'd been buried in her hot, wet pussy.

The visual alone was almost enough to make him come, but when she captured his cock in her mouth and began sucking him again, he felt the unmistakable signals of his impending climax. She kept up the assault on his senses with her hands and tongue, raising her body high enough with each stroke that his balls slipped over her creamy breasts.

She was on the upstroke when his cock erupted at last, spewing forth a fountain of cum that caught her right across her softly parted lips. With one swift motion, she came down on him, swallowing the spurts of semen as she sucked his cock deeply into her mouth. Ben gazed at her, catching the satisfied gleam in her eyes as she glanced up at him before his head sank back into the pillow.

Most men had to beg for that kind of attention, and he hadn't even had to make the suggestion. Ben allowed himself a short time to savor the moment of sated bliss, but the need to kiss and lick every inch of her delicious body was too strong to be denied. Pushing the pillow out from beneath him, he sat up and pulled her into his arms, kissing her with a hungry passion that had them both gasping for breath. Her arms surrounded him with warmth, her hands caressed his skin and delved into his hair, and her lips set his body aflame.

Ben lay down, taking her with him and then rolling her onto her back. The soft swell of her breasts and her pregnant belly reached out to him on a basic, primal level. She was his mate, the mother of his child, and the love of his life. His to love and protect and cherish.

This time, he'd gotten it right.

His kisses roamed over her body; sometimes making her moan, sometimes making her giggle, but always giving him the sense that they were welcomed, rather than merely tolerated. Her breasts beckoned to him, and he licked their creamy curves and dark pink nipples, delighting in their softness. Her sighs and moans drove him on, kissing his way over the smooth rise of her abdomen where their child was growing. He paused there, whispering assurances of his love and devotion before moving on. By the time he reached the apex of her thighs, his cock was as hard as it had ever been. No, he wasn't finished for the night, not by any means.

Kissing her pink pussy lips, he parted them with his tongue, tasting her wet sweetness as he found the firm nub of her clitoris. Her scent curled through his head, igniting a flame deep inside him. Before the night was over, he would make love to her in ways she'd probably never even thought of. An array of images raced through his mind as he licked her. Even knowing he had a lifetime to love her, he was still anxious to show her all the ways he could pleasure her, longing to make her writhe and moan until she cried out in ecstasy.

He circled her clit with the tip of his tongue, her sighs driving him on. "Do you like that, Terri?"

"Oh, yeah." Her voice was barely a whisper. "Don't stop."

"Don't worry. I won't."

She was so slick and delicious, he didn't need any encouragement. It was like finding the source of love, happiness, and pleasure all in one warm, wet spot. She wasn't holding anything back, either. Her body, her voice, the way her fingers clutched at his hair—it was all so real, so genuine. Nothing forced or feigned. She was so unlike Jackie, she might as well have been from a different planet.

He raised his head. "I just thought of something. Jackie's an alien. It's the only explanation."

Terri nodded. "She's a pod person. I'm sure of it."

"So glad we agree."

She giggled as he went down on her again. This time he didn't come up for air until her body contracted in orgasm.

"Oh, my God! You've got to feel this!" She grabbed his hand and placed it on her stomach.

She felt so tight, his first thought was that she'd gone into labor. "Does it hurt?"

"No," she gasped. "It's not a labor pain. It's one gigantic orgasm." She drew up her knees and rolled onto her side. "Oh, *wow…*"

Ben crawled up behind her. Enfolding her in his arms, he planted a kiss on her cheek as his cock slid over her wet pussy. He wanted to plunge into her, but there was something else he wanted even more. "Is it okay if I just hold you for a little while?"

She combed her hair back with her fingers. "Sure. I may need a little time to recover from that anyway."

"Take all the time you like, 'cause, baby, you ain't seen *nuthin'* yet."

"Which is why I need to rest for a minute."

"No problem." He snuggled up against her, loving the way her body spooned up against his. "I know it sounds weird, but I haven't done *anything* with a woman in so long that just being together— even when we were fighting—was wonderful. I haven't done anything pleasant with Jackie in forever, and I—maybe I should have tried harder, or done more—but she, well, she told me a while back that she didn't care if she never had sex again as long as she lived. Let me tell you, once you've heard that from your wife, there isn't much else you figure she wants to do with you, so I haven't bothered to try for a long time now. I don't know what made me horn in on her trip last summer, but I sure am glad I did."

Chapter 23

Terri knew *exactly* what made him do it. Her evil genie had evidently been working overtime, making Ben rise to the bait Terri had dangled in front of him by putting that fateful call through to Jacqueline.

And because of that one wicked little impulse, I'll never have to deal with her again. Even though she was still reeling from the shock, she had sense enough to realize she might have been a bit hasty. Granted, she had a fair amount of money saved up and was relatively frugal as a rule, but quitting her job meant that she would have to count on Ben for at least *some* support. Since she'd left home, she'd never relied on anyone. Ever. What if he changed his mind? "You're sure you want to do this? Get married? Have kids?"

"Absolutely." Taking her hand, Ben turned her toward him for a kiss. He'd apparently paid attention to her instructions because his kisses were softer, deeper, and Terri melted into him without hesitation. Lying in bed and kissing Ben… It was the sort of thing she'd been dreaming about for months. They weren't at odds with one another, and there was no one else who might arrive to interrupt them. She had all the time in the world to show him just how much she wanted, needed, and loved him. There were no secrets between them—at least, she didn't *think* there were.

She pulled away from him, breaking the kiss. "Tell me everything. I want to hear everything you've ever done, every dream you ever had. I've got a lot of catching up to do."

Ben seemed pleased at first, but then shook a knowing finger at her. "You just don't want to have to say anything yourself. Do you?"

"There's really not much to tell," Terri said candidly. "I promise you'll hear it all eventually, but for now, I believe I'd much rather listen. I like hearing your voice."

"Even when we're making love?"

"*Especially* then." Her eyes sparkled with genuine enthusiasm. "I want you to tell me what you like so I can do it over and over and over again. I want to hear you make lots of those funny little noises, too. I love that."

The smile she received from him then was worth all the pain she'd endured to get it there. *Almost.* She was happy, of course, but she still thought she would enjoy sticking an arrow or two into Cupid's chubby little butt, just so he would understand what he put people through.

"As long as it doesn't hurt, I don't care what you do," Ben said with a heartfelt sigh. "Just promise me you won't ever stop."

"Okay."

"That's it? Just 'okay'?"

"Uh-huh."

"Forever?"

"Uh-huh."

"Starting right now?"

"Sure."

"Ooh, *baby,*" he growled. "Let me have it!"

He wouldn't know what hit him. If nothing else, Chris and Joey would have been proud. She pushed him onto his back and wrapped her hand around his cock. He hadn't been kidding about his turnaround time, either. His dick was astonishingly hard and oozing syrup like an overturned bottle of Mrs. Butterworth's. Terri coated the shaft with his fluid and then climbed up on him to add her own juice. She sat down facing away from him, straddling his right leg as she eased his magnificent cock into her body. Stretching her arms above her head, she fucked him slowly, deliberately, prolonging the stroke, almost allowing him to escape before capturing him once again.

Ben was making some truly marvelous noises. Terri glanced over her shoulder just as his eyes rolled back in his head and his mouth fell open. "Feel good?"

He was staring up at the ceiling, his voice was the merest whisper. "You have *no* idea."

"Oh, I believe I do." She leaned forward, altering the angle, squeezing his dick with her strong inner muscles. "Better?"

"Mmm…yeah. *Too* good. You're gonna make me come."

"That's the whole point, isn't it?"

"I guess so. If you insist."

"I do. I'm gonna fuck you until you explode like the Fourth of July."

Ben gulped in a huge breath. "Terri…*please.*" He sounded quite desperate.

Terri smiled wickedly. "No mercy, Ben. Open your eyes. You don't want to miss this." Sitting up straighter, she scooped up her breasts, circling her nipples with her fingertips until they were every bit as hard as his cock. "Mmm…feels so good."

"Oh, God, Terri," he groaned. "You're killing me."

She reached between her legs, dabbling her fingers in her slick secretions. "Feels better when they're wet, though." With a giggle, she added, "I haven't done any finger painting in ages."

As she rotated toward him, making sure he could see her glistening nipples, Ben made the most interesting sound yet, sort of a combination between a moan, a groan, and a yelp.

"Do you like that, Ben?"

"Mmm…yeah. I'd rather suck them, though." He thrust his hips upward, driving his cock in deeper and sending waves of pleasure rippling through her body. "I want to fuck you too."

Terri laughed. "Details, dear. I want details."

"You want details? Okay, you got 'em. I want to roll you onto your back, put a pillow under your butt, get up on my knees, put your feet up on my shoulders, stick my dick in your hot, wet pussy, and fuck you 'til you scream."

The glint in his eyes assured her that this was no idle promise. Terri quivered with anticipation. "Ooh! Those are some very *hot* details."

He grinned. "Thought you'd like them."

"Something tells me we'd better make a run to the store for some cranberry juice."

Ben burst out laughing. "Of all the things to say…"

"Prevents bladder infections. Chris and Joey swear by it."

"And they would know." It was a testament to Ben's confidence—and possibly his gratitude—that he didn't mention hunting the guys down and doing nasty things to them. Terri's only hope was that they never tried to look her up—at least not for another twenty years or so. "Well, we can't have that, can we? I promise I'll go get some. Right after I make you scream."

"Go for it."

Ben carried out the "details" in less time than it had taken to describe them, but the initial penetration felt so damn good he pulled out completely a number of times just so he could plunge back into her welcoming warmth. She was tight and slick and beautiful and, above all, she was *his*. He'd nearly lost it while she was playing with her nipples, and now that she held his dick in such a firm hug, it would take some serious control to keep his promise to her.

The only trouble was, he didn't *want* to control himself. He'd been denying his needs and feelings for so long, he wanted to unleash his passion and fuck her with total abandon. Then he could make gentle love to her while he gazed into her eyes. He reminded himself that he had forever, but the need was too strong.

She fit him perfectly, and though he started slow, he picked up speed until her lush breasts were rocking back and forth with the rhythm he set. His nuts tightened. If he hadn't been able to see her, he might have lasted longer, but he couldn't make himself close his eyes. He wanted to see what he was doing to her—wanted to see the soft swell of her belly, the satisfied curl of her lips, the adoration in her eyes.

No woman had ever looked at him that way. He felt as though

an arrow had struck him in the heart, and her love was the only thing keeping him from bleeding to death. He kept rocking into her, somehow knowing that if he reached in far enough, kept going long enough, he would find her love.

Soon her breathing became erratic, her soft moans and sighs adding fuel to the fire inside him. He watched as her eyes grew round with wonder and felt her inner muscles begin rippling over his cock as she let out a climactic cry. With one final thrust, Ben's head snapped back and his body ignited.

Letting her legs down, he leaned forward, resting his hands on either side of her face. If her pregnancy had been more advanced, he might not have been able to do it, but he lowered his head and kissed her. She tasted like joy. "I love you, Terri. Have you figured that out yet?"

She nodded. "And I love you." Her sensuous lips curved into a wistful smile. "I told Joey that once, but I added your name in my head. He might not have heard it, but I still think he knew."

"Smart guy."

"Actually, Chris was the smart one, but Joey had the feelings right. He was very sweet."

Ben kissed her again. "Any regrets?"

She shook her head. "No, but I've missed them a lot over the past few months. Especially since I didn't think you wanted to have anything to do with me. I was very lonely."

Ben watched as her eyes filled with tears, cursing himself for causing her sadness. "You'll never be lonely again, Terri. I can promise you that."

"Neither will you."

Ben's own eyes were stinging with tears. "I'll do my best to deserve you. I know a lot of guys say they'll do anything for their wives, but most of them don't mean it. I do."

Terri shrugged. "That shouldn't be too hard. It's not like I'll ever ask you to fight off alien invaders or buy me a yacht."

Despite the serious tone of their discussion, the corner of Ben's mouth twitched into a smile. "You might be surprised."

"No, really," she insisted. "Even Chris and Joey said I was easy."

Anger surged through him. "You are not!"

Terri put a hand on his chest. "Not *that* kind of easy. They meant easy to please. Apparently their other 'ladies' were more...difficult."

This sounded interesting. "Other ladies?"

"That's what they do. When they go on vacation, they look for a woman who isn't having much fun, and they try to change that."

Ben winced. "I'm not sure I want to hear this."

"Oh, there's sex involved, of course, but they said they'd take me to any restaurant I liked and would take me parasailing or snorkeling or whatever else I wanted to do—although I'm sure there was a limit on how much they had to spend."

Ben was smiling again. "And what did you ask for?"

"Jalapeño poppers."

"I think I can handle that."

"Glad to hear it. Chris and Joey were a little funny about it. They took me out for Italian food the first time—said they didn't want me sucking their dicks after eating jalapeños."

"Wusses."

Terri grinned. "I've been craving poppers like crazy lately."

"Symptom of pregnancy?"

"Maybe, but I've always liked them." Her stomach let out a growl. "Can we get some now?"

"Anytime you like."

"Can I still suck your dick after I eat them?"

"Absolutely. Can't have you thinking I'm a wuss."

"No danger of that." She paused for a moment. "Although, I do remember hearing about a guy who'd been sampling some habanero pepper sauce—you know, the kind where more than one drop is practically enough to kill a person? He had to drink about a gallon of water after tasting it, and apparently he still had some sauce on his fingers when he used the restroom. Later on, his wife found him in the bathroom with his penis stuck in a glass of ice water. Said it felt like it was on fire."

Ben was almost afraid to ask. "Do *you* like habanero sauce?"

She shook her head. "Nope. Too hot."

"Thank God. Not sure I could take that."

Her lips twitched into a smile. "Wuss." She pulled him down for a kiss that thrilled him every bit as much as the first one had.

"As long as I'm *your* wuss, I can live with that." *A lifetime of Terri's kisses…definitely something to look forward to.*

"Me too."

"You remember what happened the last time you said that, don't you?"

She nodded. "I got nailed."

"Want to get nailed again?"

"Sure."

There was just one little problem with that. "Um…can you give me ten minutes?"

She shook her head. "No, but I *will* give you the rest of my life."

As Ben gazed into her captivating blue eyes, he knew he'd finally found a woman to love and a place to call home. "How about if I trade you the rest of mine?"

Smiling, she reached up to caress his cheek. "That sounds fair."

"Best deal *I'll* ever make." He turned his head, pressing his lips against her palm. "The most fun, too."

"That was only the beginning." Her eyes took on a mischievous gleam as she wrapped her legs around his waist and squeezed. "Trust me, you ain't seen *nuthin'* yet."

He laughed wickedly. "Neither have you."

"What do you m—?"

Ben shifted his position and had the pleasure of seeing her eyes roll back in her head.

"Ohh…*wow*… Hey, I thought you said you had to wait ten

minutes. Do you always overestimate like that?"

"Of course. How else can I hang onto my reputation as the best lover you've ever had?"

"Wait a minute…that sounds familiar." Her eyes narrowed. "You've been watching *Star Trek*, haven't you? Scotty *always* multiplied his repair time estimates by three. Made him seem like more of a miracle worker."

"Guilty as charged." Arching his back, he tried another angle and picked up the pace. Her soft sighs drove him on. "How about you? Ready to put this planet behind us?"

She gave him a firm nod. "Prepare to leave orbit, Mr. Tremaine."

"Aye, Captain." Ben gulped as she tightened around his cock. "Destination?"

"The stars, Mr. Tremaine. The stars."

As his eyes drank in her blissful expression, Ben smiled, knowing his life would never be the same again. And that was a good thing. A *very* good thing. "Warp speed?"

"Oh, *yeah…*"

About the Author

A native of Louisville, Kentucky, Cheryl Brooks is a former critical care nurse who resides in rural Indiana with her husband, two sons, two horses, four cats, and one dog. Her **Cat Star Chronicles** series was first published by Sourcebooks Casablanca in 2008, and includes *Slave, Warrior, Rogue, Outcast, Fugitive, Hero, Virgin, Stud, Wildcat,* and *Rebel.* Her self-published works include *Sex, Love, and a Purple Bikini* and *Midnight in Reno.* She has also published *If You Could Read My Mind* writing as Samantha R. Michaels. As a member of *The Sextet*, she has written several erotic novellas published by Siren/Bookstrand. Her **Unlikely Lovers** series includes *Unbridled, Uninhibited, Undeniable,* and *Unrivaled.* Her other interests include cooking, gardening, singing, and guitar playing. Cheryl is a member of RWA and IRWA.

You can visit her online at www.cherylbrooksonline.com or email her at cheryl.brooks52@yahoo.com

Other Titles by Cheryl Brooks

Cowboy Delight
Cowboy Heaven
Unbridled: Unlikely Lovers Book 1
Uninhibited: Unlikely Lovers Book 2
Undeniable: Unlikely Lovers Book 3
Unrivaled: Unlikely Lovers Book 4
The Cat Star Chronicles: Rebel
The Cat Star Chronicles: Wildcat
The Cat Star Chronicles: Stud
The Cat Star Chronicles: Virgin
The Cat Star Chronicles: Hero
The Cat Star Chronicles: Fugitive
The Cat Star Chronicles: Outcast
The Cat Star Chronicles: Rogue
The Cat Star Chronicles: Warrior
The Cat Star Chronicles: Slave
The Cat Star Chronicles Bundle: Slave, Warrior & Rogue
Sharing (Sextet Anthology)
Entanglements (Sextet Anthology)
Occupational Hazards (Sextet Anthology)
Mistletoe & Ménage (Sextet Anthology)
Dirty Dancing (Sextet Anthology)
Small, Medium, & Large (Sextet Presents)
The Lady Takes a Pair (Sextet Presents)
A Tale of Two Knights (Sextet Presents)
Midnight in Reno
If You Could Read My Mind (writing as Samantha R. Michaels)

www.ingramcontent.com/pod-product-compliance
Lightning Source LLC
Chambersburg PA
CBHW060148130626
46556CB00006B/2546